S0-ADQ-214

THE
LIGHT WITHIN

God's peace!
Rebecca L Matthews
Soulfest 2014
8/8/14

Rebecca L. Matthews

THE
LIGHT WITHIN

a novel

TATE PUBLISHING & *Enterprises*

The Light Within
Copyright © 2011 by Rebecca L. Matthews. All rights reserved.

No part of this publication may be reproduced, stored in a retrieval system or transmitted in any way by any means, electronic, mechanical, photocopy, recording or otherwise without the prior permission of the author except as provided by USA copyright law.

This novel is a work of fiction. Names, descriptions, entities, and incidents included in the story are products of the author's imagination. Any resemblance to actual persons, events, and entities is entirely coincidental.

The opinions expressed by the author are not necessarily those of Tate Publishing, LLC.

Published by Tate Publishing & Enterprises, LLC
127 E. Trade Center Terrace | Mustang, Oklahoma 73064 USA
1.888.361.9473 | www.tatepublishing.com

Tate Publishing is committed to excellence in the publishing industry. The company reflects the philosophy established by the founders, based on Psalm 68:11,
"The Lord gave the word and great was the company of those who published it."

Book design copyright © 2011 by Tate Publishing, LLC. All rights reserved.
Cover design by Blake Brasor
Interior design by Christina Hicks

Published in the United States of America

ISBN: 978-1-61777-134-7
1. Fiction / Family Life
2. Fiction / Christian / General
11.04.02

I thank God for his guidance, strength,
and unconditional love.

I dedicate this book to my husband, Chris,
who has been a true gift from God.

chapter 1

She sat there hunched and crying, ashamed and broken. Fallen to her knees, curled up tight, she held her wet face in her hands. When she was a child, covering her eyes had ensured that she was invisible to the monster, but this time the ugly demon was within and therefore too close to be anything but exposed.

Autumn's cold crept all around her, yet she refused to raise her eyes. She prayed for life to cease. And cease it would, as it had been known to her.

The night closed in. The darkness engulfed her. The road was deserted, and she was alone, as she had wished.

She sat back on her heels and looked around. No audience was there to feel sorry for her, and within she felt different about the hurts that sent her walking the deserted road on this dark night. Instead of the usual judgment and anger toward her husband, she felt shame at a role she was now realizing she'd played in the night's events, perhaps in much of the drama of her life.

It had seemed simple enough, Judy reflected. Just a little help at home was all she was asking for. Why was that so difficult?

She'd had a hard day at work. So many people waited for the last minute to pay their bills, which made the mailroom crazy the first week of every month. Even the fifteen minutes she worked past quitting time didn't make her feel any more caught up than she had felt first thing in the morning.

After arriving at her house and slamming the car into park, Judy dashed onto the front porch and met Sarah, the kids' babysitter, at the door.

"Sorry for being late. I tried to rush."

"No problem. I knew you'd be along soon." Sarah didn't seem irritated, though she did appear ready and waiting to leave. "The kids are in the family room watching TV."

"How were they today?"

"Oh, you know," Sarah answered with a shrug of her shoulders.

Judy did know. Jamie and Peter were a handful. One would think at the ages of thirteen and ten they would be more mature, get along better, or ignore each other altogether. But no, they fought and teased mercilessly. It wore Judy out. She hated to admit it, but she loved her job, if for no other reason than for its therapeutic properties because it offered a respite from home.

"Thank you. I really do appreciate you watching them for me after school each day."

"That's okay. I get my homework done. It gives me something to do." She stepped out the door onto the front porch and waved good-bye.

It was dinnertime, half past six, and Judy had no idea what to get the kids to eat. She stepped into the family room to say hi and stopped short. There were candy wrappers spilling off the coffee table, two empty bowls laced with ice cream residue, and a large bowl half filled with popcorn, the rest of which was strewn about the floor. The kids were sprawled out on the couch cushions, which had been taken off the couch and stacked up on the floor.

Judy was tired and irritated as she spoke. "Anybody hungry for dinner?"

"Nope," the kids answered in unison.

Peter looked up and, taking the lollipop out of his mouth, greeted his mother. "Hi, Mom." Just as quickly Jamie kicked him. "Ow!" He immediately rubbed his sore leg.

"Shh, I can't hear the show."

Judy shook her head slowly in disbelief. *How can this be?* she wondered as she turned and left the room. She couldn't make them respect each other, and they obviously didn't respect her. Fighting the temptation to begin screaming at them for their obvious screwed-up behavior, she opted to try to relax and called Rich, her husband, instead.

"Hi, honey. I just got home and wondered if you'll be here for dinner tonight."

"No, not tonight," Rich answered quickly.

"Are you sure? The kids aren't hungry. What would you like? I'll cook." Judy felt as though she was begging, and that wasn't sitting right in her gut.

"No. Really, I've got a lot of work to do here." Rich was insistent, which was just the trigger Judy needed.

"Okay. You know what? I'm sick of living like this!" She could feel her temper rising along with her voice. "I worked hard all day too, but I come home and deal with these rotten kids. Don't you think it's time you helped out around here too?"

There was silence on the phone line, but only briefly. "Okay, Judy. If it will make you happy, I'll come home for dinner. I don't really care what you cook. Anything will be fine. I'll be there in about half an hour."

Rich's calm tone did nothing to ease Judy's mood. She hung up the phone and went to rummage in the refrigerator. Upon opening the refrigerator door, she saw what looked like juice spilled throughout. The condiments were all sitting in a puddle of red, which was still dripping down the back wall and forming a pool under the see-through crisper.

Judy gritted her teeth, but even that could not contain the wail that came up from deep within her. "Jamie! Peter! Who made this mess?"

REBECCA L. MATTHEWS

Rolling her eyes and balling her fists, she felt as though she might explode. The kids were heard running up the stairs, giggling loudly as they went. Suppressing the urge to follow but fearful of her own actions, Judy focused her aggression on the task before her. She pulled all the contents out of the refrigerator, dripping juice all across the floor as she loaded them on the table. The liquid that laced the bottom of the jars and bottles now was spreading across the table to engulf Peter's school field-trip forms, yesterday's mail, and the pictures she took of some beautiful foliage, which she had printed to show Kasey at work. Judy was grabbing towels and muttering angrily as she rushed around the kitchen chaotically.

Rich stepped in the door, none the wiser. Immediately Judy snapped her attention on him. "See what the kids have done? Like I don't have enough to do around here? Do you think I need to clean up messes like this?"

"What happened?" Rich asked as he stood in the entryway looking in.

"How should I know? Nobody has admitted anything to me!" She waved an angry finger toward the family room. "They ran in the opposite direction when I asked!"

"Do you want some help?" Rich took a timid step toward the table and picked up a dripping newspaper.

Judy looked at the paper then at Rich's face. She was breathing heavily, and her face was red. "Don't just stand there letting it drip! Get something to clean it up. You are such an idiot!" She threw an already stained and wet hand towel in his general direction. It landed on the floor by his feet.

Rich put the paper back down on the wet table. He looked at his wife with an expression of amazement, which further infuriated her.

"What? What? Okay then, don't bother helping. Just stand there like an idiot and stare at me!" Judy resumed her frantic attempts at cleaning up the mess while continuing to mutter under her breath.

Rich walked through the room to get away from the situation but paused momentarily at the doorway. "You are a piece of work, Judy. You really are."

His words hurt, and in response she turned and charged at him, stopping short by a foot. She spoke through clenched teeth as she fought back the tears that threatened to show her weaker side. "Do you really think so? Well, why don't you take care of things around here for a change then? I'm done!"

Judy turned and stormed back through the kitchen and out the front door, leaving Rich to care for the kids and the house on his own.

It was dark as she drove away, yelling at the emptiness around her. She drove aimlessly as the uncontrollable tears blurred her vision. She screamed out at all the hurts and frustrations that made her hate being home.

Now, hours later, as she sat reflecting on tonight's fighting, she felt clarity taking hold.

Makeup was smeared on her face, the face she applied for her audience. It was part of her image, an image meticulously tended. She was loved and sought out by many, yet they never really knew her. They laughed at her quips and comments about others' failures. Oh, she was funny. They had compassion for her frustrations and offered her advice and help, which she never accepted. *Pride,* she called it, a play by the martyr in reality.

Within the walls of their house, her husband and children had a different view of Judy. This had always made her angry. She felt constant irritation toward those she believed encouraged her worst to show.

It was what she chose to be that fed this very attitude. The overscheduled lifestyle that brought her much praise by outsiders always left her short on time and short on patience at home and with herself. Her insides constantly churned with anxiety, stress, and fear. It seemed the simplest of matters, if not played out as she planned, would threaten to push her over the edge.

She was envied by many, yet she was her own failure. The energies spent, the sleep lost, the love now seemingly nonexistent, all cloaked her in darkness. She was ready to give up, for try as she might, things didn't seem to be turning out as she had wanted.

She had done everything for her family. She did the laundry, the cooking, and the cleaning. The kids didn't have to lift a finger. She ran all the errands and held a full-time job. No matter how much she did for her family, they did not seem to appreciate her or her efforts.

She wiped her cheeks, feeling chilled as the night wore on, but was not ready to rise and face the messy home life she had just run from. She felt compelled to remain, so she leaned against the trunk of the nearest tree and pondered the odd sensation that was now filling her in her darkest moment—peace.

It was not a familiar sensation to her and could only be explained as emptiness—yet not empty at all. In fact, it was quite the opposite. It was a fullness that pushed out all thoughts, concerns, and fear. It left just being.

Not wanting this sensation to disappear, she sat quietly and, closing her eyes, breathed slowly, in and out, in and out. Chills ran down her spine, and she felt almost giddy.

Oddly enough, she had a sense of what this was. This was how powerful and ever present God was. That still, small voice was now able to pierce her darkness. She finally had reached the end of herself, and there he was.

A memory, a time when Judy was a child, popped into her head. Her best friend had attended Sunday school every week. Judy had spent many weekends at her house, so she was exposed to the wonderful stories of the Bible they taught in those classes. She thought back to those stories now. Only bits and pieces could be conjured up in her mind, but Judy was sure there were messages within those stories that could prove quite helpful now. Perhaps the peace she had always sought for her home life would be found there, rather than in her own futile efforts.

After some time, Judy rose, and shedding the ashes of her life, she walked back down the road with a new outlook and great hope. She felt unbeatable. After a quarter-of-a-mile hike in the moonlight, she climbed into the car she had abandoned. She sat there quietly then spoke in a hushed tone, "You have me on unfamiliar ground. I feel like a different person. Nothing has changed, but everything has changed. Help me to hold on to this peace, to you, as I return home to my screaming kids and frustrated husband."

Judy felt his peace wrap around her in response. She chuckled quietly at the thought that she had just traded her heavy load for this lightweight cloak of protection. It seemed quite unfair, but she knew she needed it to walk back in the door.

chapter 2

The house was dark and quiet now. Many hours had gone by since she had run away, quite immaturely, now that she thought about it. Judy entered quietly and found her way to the bathroom, gently closing the door behind her. After cleaning up, she settled onto the couch in the family room for the remainder of the night.

She was nervous yet excited as dawn arrived upon her house. Unable to sleep, she anxiously awaited the buzzing of alarms and the shuffling of sluggish feet.

Rising early, she made a pot of coffee and rustled through the cluttered bookshelf to locate a Bible she was sure had been there. After finding it, she went to the kitchen to read, where she noticed the clean table. She opened the refrigerator and found it also very clean and nicely organized. Though a tinge of guilt pulled at her, she smiled at what her husband had accomplished.

Now Judy settled at the table. With her mug in hand and the Bible open, she sipped while she read.

The coffee seemed exceptionally good that morning, and she was thankful for the added lift it brought. Judy flipped through pages, reading bits and pieces. She was searching for a familiar story, any familiar story from her childhood. In her distraction she failed to hear Rich's footsteps as he entered the room.

Judy was caught off guard and suddenly felt nervous. "Thank you for cleaning up last night." Her voice was timid and searching.

Judy caught his quick glance before he turned away and made himself busy, too busy, pouring his first cup of coffee. She watched for a moment in silence but felt compelled to go to him.

She laid her hand on his arm. When his eyes met hers, she smiled, offering compassion and love, something she had not offered in many years. She could understand his confusion.

Their fight last night had been nothing unusual, which in itself wasn't good. Each argument resembled the ones before, all leading to the same put-downs and feelings of disgust. Why did marriage so often come to this?

She faced him now, the scent of bold coffee wafting all around them. With a timid smile, she apologized.

"I'm sorry about last night. I was wrong and realize I've been wrong for a long time." Unfamiliar tears of humbleness filled her eyes.

As Rich looked at Judy, his brows furrowed a bit. *What is he feeling?* Judy wondered. *Is it distrust? Or perhaps disgust? Maybe even disbelief?* He averted his eyes, breaking the moment.

She continued, "I don't know how, but I want to be a better wife and mother. I feel I've been treating you and the children badly. I want all of you to know I love you. I wish it could show in my actions and words as well." She sniffled as a tear slipped down her cheek.

He turned back toward the mug of coffee he had just poured. She noted that it was the mug she had given to him on Father's Day ten years ago after Peter, their second child, was born. On it was a picture of Judy cuddling with both their newborn son and his new big sister. Happy Father's Day was scrawled across the opposite side, written childishly and beautifully by their then three-year-old daughter, Jamie. Life had been difficult then. Judy remembered how she had constantly pointed out his mistakes. It was no wonder that he shrank away from his roles as father and husband.

Her thoughts returned to last night's fight, and she honestly couldn't come up with a source for the argument. Last night's issues, the kids, the mess, the disconnect, were normal. It seemed as though their life together had become one long fight with occasional breaks of uncomfortable quiet. Rich looked back at Judy. Her apology did not seem to spark any hope, though he did appear surprised by it. Apologies were not something she easily had offered in the past, at least not without sarcasm.

Judy awkwardly continued, "I did a lot of thinking last night, and though I can't explain it, I feel like I've had a breakthrough of sorts. It's like I'm being given a second chance and a new perspective on my life and who I want to be. I do love you and want you to know that I am truly sorry."

He looked down at his wife and gave her a quick kiss on her cheek. "It's okay." His response sounded empty, but he held her arm briefly as he pushed past her, leaving the room. She could feel the distance he seemed to keep hold of, and disappointment filled her heart.

Judy's attention was caught by Jamie, who came running into the kitchen with Peter on her heels, crying and grabbing at her. Judy swung around in the children's direction. "What's going on?"

"Jamie took my brush, and I need it!" Judy could see the smug grin on Jamie's face as she turned and tossed the brush to the ground just beyond Peter's reach.

With a quick, well-recognized rise of irritation, Judy had to take a breath to refocus and calm down. "Why are you instigating trouble, Jamie? Why can't you leave your brother alone?"

With a jerk, pulling her nose up to the air, Jamie stormed back out of the kitchen.

Turning to attend to Peter, Judy found he had scampered away, leaving the brush behind. It struck Judy that the game had been played on her, and she wondered at how many times in the past ten years she had been the center of such a senseless conflict.

Suddenly she became aware, vividly aware, of the roles she herself had crafted.

Disappointment consumed her. Returning to her cup of coffee, she felt her new life was barely within reach. Already, in the matter of fifteen minutes of being with her family, she had struggled to remain calm. There had been no obvious acceptance from her husband, and her children cared nothing for her love. Had they only desired to play her the fool?

She felt quite alone. Internally, Judy felt a tug and remembered where to turn. She held tightly to God within and again felt his peace crowd out her feelings of frustration. She felt his encouragement and pondered on the thought that the journey, not the destination, would garnish the greatest rewards. She had made the first step, and though the obvious results might not have been what she would have hoped for, she did not know what God was working on behind the scenes.

This realization gave her peace and a sense of freedom. She was free to follow her heart, to make steps she felt led to take, trusting that God was with her regardless of how things looked outwardly. She returned to her seat at the table and resumed her browsing over a second cup of coffee before getting dressed for the day.

chapter 3

Throughout the day, Judy pondered on her home life. Already she was seeing the error of her ways and the depth to which it had harmed her family. Guilt threatened to fill her heart. Words meant to hurt her husband kept repeating in her mind. *You're an idiot! Why are you so lazy? What kind of a father are you? I can't believe I married you.* She desperately hated what she was like. She felt compassion for her husband suddenly in a way she never had. It was crippling for her to realize that an enemy had been hurting him and that the enemy had been her. How could she have been so vicious?

She had spent years beating Rich down, and when he responded by pulling back, she turned to accusations of him not caring for or loving her. What a cycle of harm she had wrought. He could not win. She could see that now. She had been a weapon for evil. This was hard to face, but it was necessary in order to grow and change.

After years of this behavior, seemingly a lifetime, how could she rectify the situation?

After pondering on the negatives long enough, Judy changed gears and tried to focus on some goals instead. She was very busy at work, which helped a lot since her coworkers were not able to pick up on her quietness. She was able to sort mail and think, all without interruption or question.

She mentally noted some hopes. A peaceful home atmosphere and good relationships with her husband and children, these seemed the most obvious desires.

She also spent a great deal of time tossing about ideas of how these goals might be achieved. Perhaps she could visit her kids in their bedrooms to chat. She could spend time with Rich at the end of each day to touch base with how work was going.

As her work day neared its end, Judy felt herself getting excited. She looked forward to trying to put some of her ideas into action. She had hope.

That night, after Sarah was relieved of her duties, Judy got to work making dinner. Rich had come home earlier than usual, which further heightened Judy's excitement. She made a chicken stir fry, which was one of the few meals they all seemed to like.

She set the kitchen table and placed food on each of their plates. Judy called for everyone to come to the kitchen for dinner. She had prayed for direction and had imagined how it would feel to have their family united. Now she proudly and excitedly stood at the head of the table waiting to participate in the rare event of a sit-down family meal. She was smiling as her children filtered into the kitchen first.

"What's for dinner?" Peter asked.

"It's food, stupid," Jamie answered quickly with a smirk.

Peter slapped her arm then leaned over the table to see for himself. Judy's smile began to fade as she quietly watched her children. "Oh, I love stir fry."

"Good, I get the chair." Jamie grabbed a plate of food and dashed out of the room as Peter reached for a plate of food for himself.

Judy grabbed Peter by the arm to keep him from leaving. "Hold it. Jamie, get back in here!" Her temper was rising, but she was determined not to let go of her hopes just yet.

Jamie popped her head around the doorway, "What? My show is starting, and Peter had the chair earlier. It's my turn."

"I planned for us all to eat in here together. That's why I set the table this way." Judy gestured at the cups and silverware arranged neatly at each seat.

"Come on. My show is starting. I can't miss it, really, Mom." Jamie whined as if she were quite a bit younger than thirteen.

"Yeah, Mom, please? We've been waiting to see it. It's a new episode." Peter pulled free from his mother's grasp and, grabbing his plate, quickly headed for the family room.

Judy not only felt anger rising within her, but the hurt at having her hopes dashed caused her to become tearful. In frustration she began clearing away the kids' cups and napkins. "What a fool I am," she muttered under her breath just as Rich entered the room.

Judy saw Rich become tense. She turned back to the table and took a breath to calm herself. She picked up his plate and handed it to him. "It's chicken stir fry. I hope you enjoy it."

"Thank you." Rich took his plate and retreated to the living room. Judy glared at his back and, feeling the heat rise in her face, admitted defeat to herself.

Feeling as though she failed, Judy succumbed to the frustration within. Her children were so disrespectful of her, and every time she raised her voice to them, she felt miserable inside.

Though she could hear the sounds of television sets in two different directions, the kitchen felt calm and quiet. It was tranquil, as a sanctuary would feel.

There she stood, pleading her case. "God, I can't do this alone. They need to help too. Don't they?" She felt his answer and sat at the table in the quiet to absorb it.

She suddenly felt that the chaos and distance in her home wasn't her family's issue to fix, it was hers. She knew that she was seeing with fresh eyes the fruit of years of sowing bad seeds. She needed to let go. She needed to stop trying to fix it. Judy needed to focus her attention on her own relationship with God, not the relationships within the home. All else would come in due time. First and foremost was God.

Bedtime came quickly, and she was relieved as her children finally went to their rooms. The lack of sleep the night before was catching up with her. She stopped by the living room to say good night to her husband but found him dozing in his recliner, not an unusual sight. When home, he would be either there or on the loveseat in their bedroom, focused on TV until falling asleep. He would crawl into bed hours after his wife.

She looked at him and saw him differently. It surprised her as she caressed each handsome feature with her eyes. Rich was so good looking. She remembered when they were dating and recalled the complete attraction she had for him. When had she lost that feeling? The ugliness of their fighting separated them and robbed them of the passion they used to have. It dawned on her that she often did not look at him anymore really look, because of the guilt she felt from her constant nagging. She had felt it all along, the guilt, but instead of correcting the situation, she blamed him for it. She also blamed the kids and their poor behavior for her outbursts and the bad feelings she would be left with after.

Tears filled her eyes, and as her vision clouded, so did her perception. Could she really change? Was there hope for them as a family? She turned away and went to bed. Crawling under the covers, sickened by her own existence, she drifted off to a fitful sleep.

The dream, the vision, whatever it was she had, was so vivid to her. In it Judy saw an elderly woman she had known since childhood, Mrs. Bruce. Mrs. Bruce had been a substantial part of Judy's youth, but as Judy had grown into adulthood, her friend had receded into the haze of mental illness and thus was often forgotten about.

In the dream Judy couldn't help but stare with surprise at the woman before her, for not only was her friend moving about in rather normal fashion but, at such an elder stage of life, had chosen to have braces put on her teeth. Caught between confusion of what Judy was witnessing and guilt for not having maintained relations through Mrs. Bruce's difficult times, Judy chose to leave the building they were in without drawing any attention.

She was wearing braces? In judgment, Judy wondered, *Why the vanity?* It seemed so trivial after all the years lost. Surely her time would be better spent humbly reaching out to those who were hurt by her illness, her family and her friends. Judy pondered on this for a while, bothered by the selfishness of what she saw in this woman.

Sometime later in her dream, Judy returned to the same building. Upon entering she saw Mrs. Bruce dressed in a beautiful gown that flattered her thin form. She was dancing and appeared so joyful it was infectious. Judy noted that the braces had been removed, their work complete. She was radiant!

Again, Judy found herself wondering, *Why now?* What was the sense of the enjoyment she saw before her after so many wasted years? What of the family hurt by her illness? It would seem there must be something more important to address and focus attention on after coming out of a near lifetime of depression. Judy watched her; she was beautiful. Not a care in the world and so secure in herself.

It had been said by many that Mrs. Bruce had struggled with God's forgiveness. Judy had thought this strange, though, because in her better times she had stood strong by the "stripes of his blood," as she would often proclaim. It seemed odd to Judy that ultimately she might not have believed it.

But all was not as it seemed. The struggle was not with God's forgiveness of her but with Mrs. Bruce's forgiveness of herself.

It was at this late time of her earthly life that God's revelation came to Mrs. Bruce and she forgave herself completely. Suddenly she came alive to living. She didn't want to miss a thing. It wasn't vanity that drove her to straighten her smile but joy that filled her, pulling her to embrace all that this life has to offer. It mattered not the years that were lost, for life was now; the past was done. No longer would she allow self-condemnation to rob her of joy. No longer were the pains of this life able to take away her sanity. She was whole, and from the moment she chose to forgive herself, the past was no longer chained to her present or her future.

Judy woke immediately as God's message filled her heart. Now that her eyes were open to the darkness within, she was to lay her mistakes at God's feet and accept the freedom that comes with letting them go. She pondered on the things she believed and felt God continue his encouragement of her. Judy knew she must forgive herself completely, let go, and move on, and with God's help she could accomplish this.

chapter 4

As winter approached and the holiday season was getting underway, plans were being made for Jamie's fourteenth birthday. She had been born just after Thanksgiving, which was very exciting at the time of her birth. Planning a party, however, during such a busy and financially taxing time of year was often stressful.

"It's my party," Jamie firmly told her mother.

"I know it is, but it is Christmastime, and I just think a large party is too much." Judy's words were spoken softly.

Jamie crossed her arms and turned slightly away. "No."

"You're getting awfully old to be pouting like that, Jamie."

"Robin's parents let her invite thirty kids to the theater for her birthday. You just don't really care about me." Jamie glared at her mother. "What does

Christmas have to do with it anyway? It's my birthday! Why do I have to lose out?"

"Honey, I know it is an important day, but I have to say no. The expense of such a large party there is just too much for us. You can invite four friends to the movies if you want, but we won't be having a large party at the theater. We can have pizza and birthday cake at The Pizza Pub before the movie."

Jamie could sense that her argument was lost, which made her mad. "I already told everybody that we were going." The lie slipped out easily. Jamie watched her mother's face, tentatively hoping for a change of decision.

"I guess you should have made sure it was happening before you told anyone. I am sorry, Jamie. The answer is no." Judy walked out of Jamie's bedroom, gently closing the door behind her, leaving Jamie alone to face her frustrations.

Jamie had always gotten her way in the past, maybe not at first, but soon enough. All it took was some yelling, or crying, or both; she always gave in. Her mother was acting differently toward her and Peter lately. Their methods of manipulation didn't seem to work as well. Lately, when her mother said no, she pretty much meant it. They couldn't even argue the issues with her like they used to because when they tried, their mother would inevitably walk away without even so much as a raised voice.

Jamie remembered back to not long before, when she could get her mother to cry. She looked funny crying. It always brought a hidden satisfaction to Jamie. Or to make her face get beet red, that was always a sure sign that she was going to give in. Now there was no rhyme or reason, no telltale sign of which way the discussions would go. And it was irritating to be the only one getting mad.

Jamie sat on her bed thinking about her mother's suggestion. *I guess it won't be so bad*, Jamie decided. A movie night with a few friends could be fun too. She left her room to use the computer in the family room. She wanted to see what was playing at the theater on her birthday.

....

Perseverance had never been a trait of Judy's, so, for her, this was the first realization that God was truly working in her. For that, she felt encouraged. She continued her attempts at bridging the pits and valleys she had for years chiseled and worked so meticulously to create. At times, frustratingly so, she would realize how hardy the gardens of briars and thistles she had planted within them were, as they would quickly grow up to tangle through the footboards of her trestles. But persevere she did.

In the process of bridging gaps, she began to understand things differently. She began to view her husband, her daughter, and her son as the unique individuals they were.

The children's needs, hidden as they often were behind taunts and teasing, complaints and tantrums, became quite evident. With a bit of creativity and newfound patience, Judy was able to find effective ways to meet their needs or subtly dispel what they thought their needs to be. By establishing boundaries and remaining firm on decisions, she was able to alter the atmosphere of their home life quickly. The behavioral differences in the children, though small at first, became quite noticeable over time. As a result Judy's relationship with them and their relationship with each other changed significantly.

One December day, when Judy returned home from work, she was surprised to find Sarah baking with the kids.

"Wow. It smells great in here." After popping her head in the kitchen to see what the smell was coming from, Judy returned to the entryway to hang her coat and scarf, smiling to herself.

Peter came tumbling in to meet her with a cookie in hand. "Mom, Mom, you've got to try this!"

Judy took it, and while watching his face, she took a big bite. "Mmm. This is wonderful!" She draped her arm over his shoulder, and together they returned to the kitchen. "Sarah, thank you so much for doing this." Judy shared a smile with Jamie, who was wearing Judy's red and white striped apron.

"Mom, we're gonna give these cookies to our teachers as Christmas gifts tomorrow since it's the last day before Christmas vacation," Jamie shared.

"Well, we're all done here, and we've cleaned up. Kids, you've done a good job." Sarah stepped from behind the counter and joined Judy by the door as Peter returned to package their presents with Jamie.

Judy and Sarah stepped into the entryway so Sarah could get bundled up for the cold. "I can't thank you enough for all you do for us. I realize the kids are old enough to be home alone. I just don't want them to be, and they like you so much. Because of you I have been able to work without worrying about them. I really do appreciate that."

"No problem. I don't know what you've done, but they sure are so much easier to be around lately. I tend to forget that they used to fight all the time. I could never have imagined baking like we did today."

Sarah's observations brought a smile to Judy's lips. She looked in on the kids as they worked side by side chatting quietly between themselves. Judy had to agree. They were much easier to be around, which led to her next point. "Sarah, I hope this won't be a problem for you. I have prayed a lot about this decision, and after talking it over with Rich, I have decided to ask for reduced hours at work. I really would like to be here with the kids more myself."

Sarah smiled. "I can understand that." She thought for a moment then continued. "No, it won't be a problem. I'll be graduating this spring. It will give me a chance to spend more time with my friends and family before I head off to college."

"Thank you for being so understanding. In all the excitement of making this decision, I realize I hadn't thought that it might inconvenience you. I am planning on talking to Human Resources after the new year begins. I'll let you know more when I know more." Judy gave Sarah a hug then stepped back. "Again, thank you for all you've done for us."

Sarah smiled then hollered good-bye to the kids and headed out into the brisk winter air.

....

Christmas had come and gone, and Judy was able to reduce her hours at work once the new year had begun. It was late January when Judy approached Rich about Peter's upcoming birthday.

"Can you believe he's going to be eleven?" Judy asked.

Rich was sitting in his recliner in the living room watching the news when Judy sat opposite him on the couch. He thought for a minute, and his brows furrowed momentarily. "Yeah, it's amazing how quickly time flies." His voice lacked emotion, and Judy felt sad for that.

"I know. It really does fly." The atmosphere was uncomfortable. Rich didn't look away from the television at all, which made Judy feel as though she were interrupting. "I was wondering if you wanted to go shopping for him with me on Saturday. Since Sarah hasn't been watching the kids anymore, I thought it would be a good opportunity for them all to see each other again." Rich didn't answer right away, and Judy felt a bit nervous at her next suggestion. "We could make it a date." Rich did turn to look at her then, but he wasn't answering. Wringing her hands, Judy offered another option instead. "If you would rather not go, I understand. I can go myself."

"It's not that I don't want to; I thought I explained that Phil and I are trying to buy another building. I'm sure I told you." Judy's puzzled look and blushed cheeks reminded him otherwise. "I am meeting an inspector in Amesbury Saturday at the property."

"Oh. That's okay." Judy felt like an outsider in her husband's life. Her emotions were a strong mixture of anger and hurt, which she fought to suppress. "No, I didn't know." Trying to sound strong, she continued the conversation, though she was shaking a bit at this point. "What's the building for?"

"We decided to open another store. We had been talking about it for a while now since Haystacks has been doing so well. We wanted to expand by adding another store in a higher populated area, and when this building came on the market in Amesbury, it just seemed right." Rich's voice lacked emotion. His discussion sounded matter of fact, and his attention was constantly drawn back to the news.

Judy rose from the couch. "Okay. Does that mean you will be gone more than you already are?" She could hear in her own voice that she was losing control of her emotions, and before he could answer, she left the room to cry in solitude.

Conversations with Rich were infrequent and made her feel as though he was slipping farther and farther out of reach.

Through these many months of spiritual growth, Judy had come to know God's voice within and knew when to, in faith, follow his guidance. Though she wished and hoped for more positive changes in her relationship with Rich, Judy realized she needed to let go of wondering and worrying about it. She felt she needed to "live in the here and now" instead of focusing on a future goal. It was quite refreshing when the weight of this burden began to lift. No longer did she need to bear the burden of her guilt, and no longer was she consumed with constant thoughts of how to show him the "new her." She was able to simply be.

....

Having been fortunate enough to change her work schedule, much to her coworkers' shock, to more closely model her children's school schedule, she was spending a great deal more time with them.

On the night of Peter's birthday, after all the excitement had subsided, Judy sat, cross-legged, at the foot of his bed. "How was your day, honey?" They had

had a sledding party at the park, where there was a large hill, and every winter the town groomed it for sledding and kept the shed and bathrooms open so people could warm up when things got too chilly. Judy brought the cake to the shed and had all the kids meet them there.

"It was such a good day, Mom. Thank you for the party and the presents. I love the sled you got me. It went so fast." Judy smiled warmly as Peter continued his excited chatter. "None of my friends' sleds were nearly as fast as mine."

"You were fast. It scared me when you nearly ran into Cody. I was sure he wouldn't get out of the way fast enough, but he did."

"I know. Wasn't that funny?" The two laughed together at the memory.

"Well, I hope you sleep well. You have school in the morning." Judy rose from her perch and gently kissed Peter's cheek.

"Oh yeah, and thanks for the cupcakes at school. I shared them with some of the teachers too."

"You're welcome. I'm glad you had a good day." Judy shut off Peter's light and, stepping into the hall, closed the door behind her. This had been a good day. She had only wished that Rich had been able to come home earlier to enjoy the party. He was missing so much of the kids' lives. What was worse, they didn't even seem to care. She wished she hadn't pushed him away so much when they were young.

As Judy headed for Jamie's room, she realized she was no longer looking forward to bedtime to avoid the constant complaints. Boy, had things changed.

....

Judy was excited to spend time with her children and looked forward to meeting them at the bus stop at the end of each school day. After homework and snack time were done, they would often walk to the library together. The weather was getting warmer, as spring was awakening, and it was during these walks that she was able to observe the stark differences between the pair. They were simply fascinating!

Jamie was such an active girl, so full of energy. She was outgoing in ways that Judy envied. She seemed comfortable with who she was. Peter, on the other hand, enjoyed quiet times and time with his mom. He wasn't necessarily shy but seemed to like keeping to himself. They were so different now than when they were fighting and teasing each other. Perhaps it was that Judy had taken the time to get to know them.

She grabbed opportunities to encourage each child in their own personal likes. Peter had picked up a cookbook from the library, which enhanced their cooking time together. Jamie joined a dance class, and it warmed Judy's heart to hear her excitement as she practiced in the living room: these were precious times for her.

Rich remained distant, but that was okay. Judy welcomed him the nights he came home early enough and offered herself for discussion. At times he shared bits of his day; most times he remained quiet. She felt him, though—the subtle looks in her direction, the thoughtful gestures as he would pick things up from the store for her. She at times dwelled on his distance but trusted that God was big enough and powerful enough to deal directly with Rich and touch his heart in his own time. That was not her place.

chapter 5

Since she was young, Judy had struggled with obsessive traits. Organized and in control she was not; these were merely part of an image she had for years presented to the public eye to hide the truth inside. Within the walls of her home were the hidden consequences. She couldn't let go of anything over the years. Though she believed there was organization to the mess, it was overwhelming.

A book had recently caught Judy's eye at the library, so she took it home to browse. It had been a quick read, and it profoundly changed the way she saw things. It was a book on cleaning up the clutter in your life, specifically in your home. This book could have been written with her in mind. It described her house to a T.

She had large piles of used clothes upstairs, all of which she had plans for, of course. The name brand clothes were for the consignment shop, but these had to be better organized. Some clothes would go to Goodwill, and others would be perfect for her coworker's daughter or her neighbor's children. She even held on to a few just to use the fabric to make crafts for the home based on an article she'd read last year, which was in one of the many magazines she also saved. Those were piled up on the living room floor. Each time her children outgrew something or she was handed down something from a friend that her kids wouldn't wear, it was added to one of the piles. The piles grew, but the plans were as yet unrealized.

Papers were also piled about; the office was packed. There were papers to be filed, papers yet to have been gone through, pictures to organize, frame, and hang; there was schoolwork to put in the kids' bins as keepsakes. It was so overwhelming that the only use for the room now was basically the path through it to the living room.

It was increasingly clearer to Judy the work God was doing deep within her because she was becoming more able to "see" the mess she had organized around them. With this clearer vision came the realization that she had harbored guilt over these piles. She recalled snapping at Rich and the kids many times unfairly in the past in defense of the mess. The fact that her family had to live in and hide such conditions due to her own controlling behavior was sad to her.

It was Judy's procrastination that led to this orderly chaos. It came from the belief that she had to plan and complete tasks perfectly. Since she didn't have time to tackle any one project and complete it thoroughly, she could never tackle any, thus the piles. In the past she would get extremely irate if anyone shuffled through any of it. It seemed to make her feel threatened, as if her ways were being questioned or her failures pointed out. Everyone had to ask her where things were or risk getting yelled at for messing up her piles. She had been, after all, the one in control, at least in her own mind.

Having chosen to take the day off from work to address this issue now placed so strongly on her heart, Judy took a deep breath and stood in the entryway of the house. She tried to look at everything through the eyes of an outsider stopping by for a visit. What would a stranger see? She could scarcely believe what was before her.

Scanning the room, she could see the small table, which was originally meant to hold keys, a lamp, and a beautiful bouquet of fresh flowers, just as you would see in a magazine. The keys were there, next to a lamp with a torn shade and a blown bulb, as well as a screw-driver, half-opened mail dated four months ago, a sandwich bag with squished crackers and cheese (how old that was could be anyone's guess), and one ratty glove left over from winter, waiting for its mate.

A bench, meant to be a comfy spot to sit and remove boots, held piles of clean folded clothes waiting to be brought to bedrooms, a pair of snow pants ready to go in the winter storage box, and two books from the library.

The coat hooks to the left were overloaded with winter clothes that she had meant to wash and put away at the change of the season a month ago. Not to mention the trash strewn in the corners, the dust on the few bare spots of furniture, dirt on the floor, and cobwebs on the ceiling. This scene was truly an eye-opener to her.

Room by room, Judy continued the survey with similar results. Once her tour was complete, Judy leaned on the kitchen counter, directly on a sticky spot caused by last night's ice cream. Shaking her head and rolling her sleeve up past the stickiness, she thought to make a cup of tea, sit down, and begin planning. But planning, she realized, for her was merely the same old cycle of procrastination. It surely would be the beginning of the end for this day's work. Judy set about the task put on her heart instead.

Remembering the suggestions in the book, Judy grabbed a broom and headed up the stairs to work her way around the entire house, sweeping down cobwebs. When this job was complete, she stepped through each room with the trash can, grabbing anything obviously not needed. Next, she went through each upstairs room and took items off any horizontal surfaces that were not meant to be on them. She made organized piles of like and similar objects.

By now it was near lunchtime, and Judy was getting hungry. She browsed each room one final time before heading down for a quick lunch. What she saw encouraged her. The difference in these rooms was great.

Before getting food items out, she looked around the kitchen. Rushing through it, she put dirty dishes and utensils in the sink, gathered the papers from the counter into one pile, and, spraying cleaner on all the surfaces, wiped away the grease, grime, and stickiness. After a few bouts of spray and a ridiculous amount of paper towels, she looked at her work and smiled.

Now she could eat. She made herself a peanut butter and jelly sandwich, pulled out the barbecue chips, made a glass of chocolate milk, and sat down to a feast the child within her loved. She thought about the person she was becoming as she ate.

Judy pondered the changes God had made in her life. The nights of fighting with her husband had ceased, though the relationship still left much to be desired. The irritation once felt for her children had been replaced with a respect she didn't know adults could have for their kids. The stress from work she used to hold on to had dissipated.

Overall, her transformed life was so much more enjoyable. Though all the personal changes Judy experienced had been challenging, God's peace had been present, helping even the most difficult struggles seem bearable in the end. Facing the benefits of her new life brought a smile to Judy's face.

It was remarkable being on the flipside of life, beyond the chaos and anger. It was enjoyable and tranquil. She was learning constantly and trusting thoroughly. She realized that if things hadn't been so bad, she would not be nearly as appreciative as she was at this moment. *Thank you, Lord.* Silent tears slipped down her cheeks as she bowed in humble adoration.

Prior to meeting the kids at the bus stop, Judy accomplished great things. The house even smelled good. The kids loudly charged through the door but became briefly silent.

Jamie was the first to respond before disappearing to her room. "Wow! What happened here?"

"Hey, I can put my hat here!" Peter scrambled onto the bench, which was repositioned beneath the coat hooks, and placed his Red Sox cap on one of the empty hooks. After dropping his backpack on the floor, he asked, "Mom, what have you done? It looks so different in here. You must have been busy all day. It looks great!"

Peter's excitement warmed Judy's heart. She sat down beside him, smiling as she opened his Bug Juice and he began eating the Oreos she had gotten him from the cabinet. "Yes, I've had a busy day, but it's been fun." Judy realized she still had so far to go but didn't feel the old need to have everything done right now. She had a lot of time to think on today's lessons and looked forward to organizing a bit day by day. Reducing the amount of stuff they had was big on her list at this point.

Jamie sauntered back down the stairs and entered the kitchen. She sat to eat the Oreos her mother handed her and asked for a cup of milk. "Our rooms look great, Mom. Do you think I can change mine around?"

Judy could recognize the need for Jamie to be more of a decision maker in her own world. "I think a change would be great for you. Let me know if you need me to help."

Jamie looked up in surprise. "You want me to do it, by myself?"

"I have so much more to do. It would be wonderful if you could come up with your own ideas and work on it yourself. Just let me know if you need help. The bureau may be a bit heavy, but you can push it I'm sure."

Hopefully leaving her daughter feeling encouraged, Judy looked away to leave the impression it was no big deal. She had never let the kids touch anything, let alone move furniture. The realization of this was just settling in. In a matter of moments Jamie appeared very excited.

"Please make sure that homework is done first, though," said Judy, outlining their priorities.

Jamie went to the entryway, where she had dropped her backpack, and, returning to the table, settled in to attack her homework. Judy smiled.

Peter got his school books out and started his homework as well. Judy went to the living room to wrap up the latest of what she had been accomplishing before it was time to start dinner. She wondered what Rich would think when he came in. She couldn't wait to see his reaction.

chapter 6

Tacos were quick and easy. This was the perfect dinner to top off an extremely busy and rewarding day. It was the kids' favorite meal and, with no arguing, was eaten at the dinner table in the kitchen with their mother, instead of in front of the TV in the family room.

Jamie had been working on her bedroom for the past hour but took a brief respite to eat a couple well-loaded tacos. She was so excited she did not linger long at the table. Explaining that she had so much more to do, she ran back up the stairs, leaving Peter and her mother behind.

Peter was finicky and needed his taco made a certain way. Cheese was his love. Judy loaded that first onto a soft shell; a tiny hint of meat was next, followed by a scattering of lettuce. No tomato allowed. After rolling it up, Judy placed it in the microwave for a few seconds, just enough to melt the cheese. Peter enjoyed his soft taco with moans of over-exaggerated bliss.

Judy ate a couple tacos herself then began cleaning up and putting away dinner's remains. She emptied, reloaded, and started the dishwasher. Filling the sink, she washed by hand the remaining bowls and pans that didn't fit, drying and putting them away just as quickly as they were washed. Peter lingered in the kitchen. He sat at the counter and played his video game for the next hour and a half. Amazingly, following through on one thing put on her heart by God further altered the atmosphere, which was becoming home for both her and her children.

Once the dishes were done, Judy swept the kitchen floor in anticipation of mopping later. She wiped down the appliances and looked in disbelief at how homey her kitchen looked when it was clean.

"Peter, it's time for dessert. I'm going to go get your sister. Why don't you pick out the kind of ice cream you want? Grab a spoon and bowl while you're at it." Judy, having always done everything for her kids, took this moment to step out of her comfort zone and help Peter be more self-sufficient. "Don't forget the jimmies and chocolate sauce. I'll be right back."

Judy hesitantly left Peter to fend for himself and went upstairs. Jamie's bedroom door was closed. Judy reached for the doorknob but paused, choosing to knock instead.

"Uh, come in," Jamie answered timidly. Judy felt the oddity of the moment. She had never knocked before. She felt the power of the respect she had just shown her daughter.

Judy opened the door and stepped through the doorway. She was so excited by what she saw. "Wow, Jamie!" Jamie had moved her bed to the wall on the left, and though her bureau had not been moved, it was neatly organized with her personal items. Her desk, now brought beside her bed as an end table, was organized and neat as well. The trash can, borrowed from the bathroom, was full. Judy smiled. "This looks great!"

"I know," Jamie answered excitedly. "Look, I moved my clock so I can shut off the radio without getting out of bed at night."

Judy pointed as she spoke. "Oh, your shoes look great all organized like that." Turning slowly to take it all in, she continued, "I like how you set out your knickknacks. They look good on your windowsill."

"Here are some things I don't really want anymore. What should I do with them?"

Judy looked at the pile and thought of her own that she had been working on. "I'll take them with me. Good job." Every move had a purpose. Judy heard loud and clear that her daughter was maturing and knew what she needed. "I came up to let you know it's dessert time. I'm proud of you; you've done a lot." She hugged Jamie, gathered up the pile of unwanted things, and they both headed back to the kitchen. Entering the kitchen, Judy found Peter standing at the table with a bit of a pout on his face. With arms folded, he sat. "I don't know where you keep stuff in here. Where are the sprinkles?"

Judy surveyed the scene a bit more closely. There was a small scoop of ice cream in a bowl and a bent spoon on the table. That was it. "Wow, I'm sorry, guys. It's about time I share the work around here." With a chuckle, Judy left the room briefly to put Jamie's things down then returned. She opened each cupboard and drawer and explained where they could find anything, during which time Peter picked out the things he had been searching for. After straightening the spoon, Judy scooped more ice cream into his bowl then offered for Peter to finish creating his concoction. This brought the smile back to his face. He drizzled and scooped and sat to delightfully eat his dessert.

Jamie was offered a bowl and spoon and was also set free to create whatever her heart desired. They smiled at each other, mother and daughter, as Jamie added items to her dessert as well.

Judy sat down and relaxed for a while with her children as they ate. After dessert Peter and Jamie got ready for bed. She planned to continue her cleaning journey once they were tucked in. Rich would be home soon. He had been coming home late since things were getting so much busier at work.

chapter 7

The kids were in bed, the kitchen tidy, and the chairs were moved out of the room. Judy sought the mop and realized there wasn't one that worked anymore. Chuckling at the fact that she didn't even know that until now, she grabbed the mop bucket anyway. With not much searching, she retrieved an old bath towel from one of the clothing piles upstairs, found a pair of scissors, and reduced it to rags. Returning to the kitchen, Judy filled the bucket with hot water, adding a generous amount of Lysol disinfectant, and threw in a rag, setting them aside.

Grabbing the broom, Judy swept the entire kitchen a second time, reaching each corner and searching the kick space below the counters. She even took the time to move the appliances completely out of their spaces, filling the dust pan a few times more.

Returning the broom and dustpan to the closet, Judy grabbed the soap-filled bucket. Kneeling at the spot that had occupied the refrigerator, she wrung sudsy water out onto the floor. After spreading the solution around, she got up and moved to kneel where the stove had been, where she repeated the action. As the book had suggested, she left these spots soaking to loosen the grit and began hand-mopping at the farthest corner of the room. She washed in rows, scrubbing each row twice thoroughly before moving to the next. Judy repeated this process until she was nearly done with the entire kitchen floor and the appliances were returned to their original locations.

Deep in focus on the project at hand, Judy failed to hear Rich pull in. Surprised by the sound of the door closing, she looked up from her kneeling position. Her husband hesitantly entered the doorway of the kitchen. She smiled up at him, pushing the hair out of her eyes, thinking how messy and grungy she must look. "Hey, how was your day?"

"Okay." Rich looked down at Judy. "Looks like you've been quite busy. This looks great." Rich pointed as he glanced around the kitchen. "The entryway too."

His comments were well received, yet she was worried what he would feel seeing the rest of what she had been working on. Some of the house, though different, was almost messier than before. Judy voiced a statement God put on her heart for the day. "Things have to get far worse before they get better." It was repeated often in her mind, helping her to keep moving forward no matter how much worse the place seemed to be getting.

Judy stood up, stretching her legs carefully as she rose. Having been bent for so long, she felt the ache settling in. Stepping forward, she placed a kiss gently on Rich's cheek. He watched her as she stepped back. Judy could sense sadness in his demeanor. "Is everything okay?"

"Yeah, just a busy day, not as busy as yours though." Rich pointed to the work Judy had accomplished.

God had asked her to let go of her wants and just to be, which she had done for the most part. There were the occasional sleepless nights, though, and the stolen glances laced with wishes that their romance could be rekindled. She knew peace only came with obedience, and God's request of her was to let go of Rich—such a difficult thing to do.

A quick glance at the clock surprised her. It was nearly ten.

"Oh my goodness, I hadn't realized how long I've been doing this. I've got to get this done and go to bed." Judy returned to her kneeling position, though her knees protested, and to the last small stretch of flooring left to be tackled. She had a smile on her lips as Rich went to their bedroom to settle in to his nighttime routine.

....

Their bedroom was more like a suite. The space was large enough to have accommodated the bed and bureaus in one area and a loveseat, coffee table, end tables, and an entertainment center in the rest. Their bathroom was what most people only dream of having—dual sinks, separate toilet room, a shower big enough for two, and a soaking tub.

This house had been a good find when their children were young. They had needed the larger space, additional bedrooms, and yard, and money was pretty good. Their large bedroom, however, encouraged division. On the nights Rich made it there, he settled onto the loveseat to watch television, often avoiding conversation altogether. Who could blame him, though? The only chances he had to speak were his futile attempts at self defense.

Their room, over time, had become the drop-off site for anything Judy touched. Even though the room was large, there was not much space left. It certainly did not offer an atmosphere of romance. It was here that Rich entered this night and stood in awe.

Before him now, their room was clutter free, organized, and set up romantically. A feeling of loss overwhelmed him as he browsed the space. The snapshots hanging were not new but were prominent with the lack of clutter. They were wonderful pictures, framing important memories of their life together: their wedding, Judy holding Jamie as an infant, Rich helping Peter blow out the candles on his second birthday. On the bureau there were additional candid shots and candles wafting their heady scents. Confusion set in as Rich turned to see Judy standing in the doorway.

"I need a quick shower." Judy smiled toward Rich as she ducked into their bathroom, leaving the door open. He saw a hint of seduction in her look. Again, confusion tugged at him. He sank into the loveseat instead of answering her look. He felt overwhelmed; emotions had been messing with him for many months since Judy truly seemed sincere in her changes.

It had been ten years at least of nagging and fighting. He had come to feel insecure in his role as husband and father but also as a man. He had immersed himself in his work and at least felt his worth in the financial support he provided his family. His job also gave him his own space to be and portray the person he wanted to be.

He felt a connection to other men who took the "long way home," attempting to avoid the dreaded wife. He resented Judy for this. Even though it was his decision to live this way, he felt it hadn't been much of a choice at all. Judy screamed all the time, at all of them. Even if he dodged the bullet, his kids suffered as the targets. It was no wonder to him that their behavior was horrible. They were made into disgruntled, rebellious kids. Who wouldn't have rebelled? After all, that's what Rich had been doing by avoiding her.

Dramatic changes had taken place in Judy over time. It was something Rich could not have imagined witnessing, ever. He couldn't accept it at first, but months into her new personality, he could really sense the sincerity of who she was becoming. He saw her struggle for a while, attempting to remain calm, but now calmness was what she exuded. Peace pulsed through her. The changes also had touched their children. He couldn't stop feeling resentment at what he'd lost through all the prior years—the relationship he never had with his kids, the love he never shared with his wife. He shook his head while hanging on to these thoughts. Why the changes now?

Then he felt her presence. Looking up, he faced his wife, beautiful yet timid, standing in the room, her shower done. Resentment and confusion filled his heart. He knew what he had to do.

chapter 8

Timidly, Judy moved toward Rich. She had stepped forward in many ways this day, and, awkward as it was, she was doing it once again. Though she had been nervous setting their bedroom up this way, her goal was to claim it as a couple's domain, their domain. This night was the anniversary of their first date fifteen years earlier, a small detail that neither of them had acknowledged since their marriage. She'd only remembered it herself this morning when she'd cleared her schedule for the day.

God had kept her to himself for seven months now. Though she had wished for more with her husband, she had entrusted him to her Lord as he had asked. Tonight, however, she felt it was time to act.

Rich looked up but did not rise. Judy stepped closer. Her heart skipped a beat, and insecurity danced around her as she stood naked before him. She knelt down and set her hand on his knee. Her touch did not prod for attention; it merely offered a humble concern for his hesitancy. She was unsure of what was flitting behind his eyes.

He took a deep breath and, placing a hand upon hers, looked her in the eyes. "We have to talk." It was a slow statement, and it held within it the confirmation that simplicity would not be theirs tonight.

"Okay, give me a minute." Rising, Judy returned to their bathroom and dressed for bed. A prayer lingered in her mind, and she felt strength to face what she hoped would be the beginning of communication with her husband. She was so sorry for the years of pain she had brought. This seemed as though it could be her chance to offer herself, humble and truly remorseful. She felt optimistic that Rich was ready to talk, ready to listen, and ready to believe in her once again.

He was standing when Judy returned to their bedroom. She climbed onto the arm of the loveseat, ready to listen. He looked at her and sighed. "I don't know how to begin."

The moment was awkward, and Judy felt compelled to take control. "I'm so sorry, Rich, for how badly I treated you all those years. You deserved so much better. Please understand that I am ready to share a healthy relationship. Please, let's take down the walls and begin again."

She was smiling and confident. Hope filled her plea. After all, she had experienced such tremendous change; she believed all things were possible.

He could scarcely get his words out.

"Judy…" Rich turned to face her directly. "I've been in a relationship with another woman for four years." Tears filled his eyes, and his voice cracked with the confession.

The shock could not have been more overwhelming. The words suffocated her heart and sent her mind spinning in seconds flat. The hope, the confidence, the excitement—all were stifled. The dread that replaced them was heavy. Judy quickly looked away upon hearing this confession and found that she could not return her gaze to him. The self-destructive guilt of what she had created now filled the space between them and within her. Of course this would have happened. How could she not have expected, or even suspected, such a thing?

Insecurity engulfed Judy. She felt ugly. Tears filled her eyes, and she wanted nothing more but to hide. Rising, she passed by Rich to leave the room, this room she had tenderly arranged for them on this very anniversary. *What a fool.*

Rich reached for her, but she slipped past him to leave the room. She climbed on the sofa in the family room. Curled up hunched and broken, once again, just as she had on a deserted road many months prior, she sobbed.

A short time later, Rich turned the family room light on. His voice was strong, and his words were absolute. "I've packed some things. I'm not staying. I'm sorry." He turned the light off, leaving her in the dark once again as she heard the door open and close. She listened as his car started and backed down the drive. She heard the sound of his motor drift into silence, replaced by the sobbing she couldn't seem to control.

It was a sleepless night. Judy beat herself up. Eventually fear settled in. What was to happen next? Who was this other woman? Were they happy and in love? How could she handle her finances as a single mother? Divorce, visitation schedules, another woman, splitting assets—so much to worry about, and, fool that she was, she had brought this on herself.

When morning broke, Jamie and Peter bounded down the stairs none the wiser to the events of the previous evening. Judy lay an empty smile upon her children, got their breakfast, and trudged through the routine with a sense of dread tied to her every step.

She could see the confusion in the kids' eyes as she drove them to school. It made the tears threaten to come again. She wrestled her way through the morning work schedule. Her coworkers were very concerned, and come noontime, Kasey approached. "You look terrible. Are you okay?"

"I'm fine."

People tiptoed around her the rest of the day. Two thirty didn't come soon enough, but returning home to the changes she was in the midst of did nothing but compound her sadness.

The kids went to work on homework in Jamie's room. Judy heard her door close and music turn on.

They must have sensed the tension and decided to avoid it. She shouted her desperate confusion at the walls. "What was it all for, anyway? Why? Why? Why?" She sank to her knees on the fresh, clean kitchen floor, tears falling through her fingers. The sadness was so deep. The hurt was unbearable. She was not angry at Rich; she understood. She was furious with life. It had been going so well. How could it suddenly turn so bad? She was embarrassed and insecure and was getting caught up in a game of comparing herself to the elusive "other woman," who must be so perfect.

In anticipation of the kids' afternoon routine, she put snacks on the table along with a note claiming she didn't feel good and went to bed until dinnertime.

God spoke to her heart. "Things have to get far worse before they get better." She heard him repeat these words of encouragement as he had time and time again when she was sorting and cleaning. She cried all the more, slipping into a short fitful slumber.

Day after day went by with no word from Rich. Life went on the same, though completely different. Darkness crowded her thoughts, laced her actions, and dripped from her words. Sleep was becoming elusive, and as tiredness settled in, poor judgment climbed aboard. Judy began snapping at people, her children were avoiding her once again, and she began to feel much like the person she'd shed many months prior. Negativity was a weight she carried draped about her shoulders. Though the children had each asked about their father and his noted absence, she could not discuss him with them. Her halfhearted suggestions that he was busy at work didn't seem to satisfy them.

"What's wrong, Mom? You've been acting different. Are you okay?"

Jamie's questions were kind and well deserved. Her response was short. "Don't worry about me."

Jamie persisted. "I am worried, though."

"Honey, really, I'm just not feeling well. Don't worry." Judy tried to change the subject. "How is school going?"

"Well, today we got to go outside during art class, since it was so warm out."

Judy could feel her mind wandering. She was staring out the window at the sunny afternoon but couldn't feel the happiness spring usually brought to her. She realized eventually that Jamie had left the room, and though she felt bad for not paying attention to her, she could not bring herself to do anything about it.

Darkness crowded her dreams; she was not in a good space. She missed the peace that up until recently had filled her life but could not shake the thoughts that crowded out God's wisdom. *Things have to get far worse before they get better.* She held on to these words for, though they forecast doom, they promised a light at the end of this dark tunnel.

....

"I don't know, Peter. Mom just says she doesn't feel good. It does seem as though something bad has happened, but she won't talk to me about it."

"It just seems weird. I miss her smiling and laughing with us, and I wonder what is going on with Dad."

Jamie agreed wholeheartedly. "Me too."

"I suppose if it were too terrible she would have told us something." Peter thought quietly for a minute then continued, "I wonder if we should try to help out more. Maybe she really doesn't feel good. But I'm afraid that she's going to yell at me like she used to. She's starting to act like that again, and I had forgotten what that was like."

Jamie ruffled Peter's hair affectionately. "I had forgotten too." She didn't want to alarm her younger brother, but she had overheard their mother crying a lot. Jamie had spent a lot of time with Peter hoping to protect him from their mother's sadness or anger. She risked being yelled at last night by asking why Dad hadn't been around lately. All her mother could say was that he was busy at work, just as she had said before. He never was home with them much, so it made sense, but she did feel uneasy about it. Something was wrong.

"Jamie, do you want to play Monopoly with me?"

"Sure, kid. Why don't you get your pajamas on while I set up the game?" With their mother being so separate lately, Jamie stepped into her role as caretaker for Peter. It was sad, but at the same time it made her feel more grown up, and it was bringing them closer together.

chapter 9

Judy, having no facts beyond the words stated by her husband that horrid night, had allowed herself to be seduced by the shadows of darkness. Night after night she would wake filled with the dread left over from a bad dream. Quickly, though, she would realize that reality was her nightmare. Thoughts raced and conclusions were reached only to melt and alter into other illusions altogether. She felt so lonely and missed her husband and the life they had had.

The fact that their relationship had been incomplete and basically nonexistent was being replaced by exaggerated memories of the good times they had shared during their early years together. Judy remembered a picnic they had gone on. They had taken their lunches and headed out into the countryside, where they chased each other around an overgrown field. She cried now at the happiness she had lost. She thought about the nights they spent talking as they had laid on the hood of his car watching for shooting stars. They had so much to share back then.

Her anger transformed. First, she was furious for having brought Rich's infidelity on herself. She had been such a miserable person to be with. Who could blame him for having sought enjoyment in some loving relationship elsewhere? Her anger eventually turned from herself and focused on Rich. The sleepless nights had conjured many images of his lusty behavior with a mistress. She hated them both so much. Four years together—how could he have done this to her? She was sure they were thrilled at having the truth exposed and having freedom now in their grasp.

Each day was difficult to get through. Judy was putting on an act at work and avoiding the kids at home. She had yet to confront the changes looming before them. Not daring to call Rich to discuss the next step, Judy swept the baggage under the rug and chose not to tell anyone.

Demons that poked at her all through the day tumbled out of their hiding places to torment her through the nights. The irrational thoughts were as waves pounding the beach, each wave filled with what ifs, should haves, and why mes. As the storm grew, the waves also grew in size, crashing harder on the tiny, fragile pebbles that were her heart. Judy's thoughts turned to planning ahead, far beyond what reality had brought her thus far. Rather than facing the days at hand, she thought of future court hearings, visitations, loneliness, and the house; all thoughts overwhelmed and gripped her with fear. The night's tortures seemed to last so long.

To avoid the inevitable, she was staying up later, hoping the delay would ensure a deeper sleep, a sleep less inclined to be disrupted by demon hands.

Knowing all—past, present, and future—God spoke to Judy. Addressing what was specific to her needs at this time, he asked her to fast. The Holy Spirit within, though ignored for some time now, was placing his wisdom on her heart. Judy hesitated and questioned, failing to remember the peace that came with simple trust and obedience.

She pondered on fasting as it was used for dieting and as it was used as a religious custom. In matters of health, Judy never felt it right to withhold food for vanity's sake. Being unclear on the religious aspect, she reached for her Bible. Browsing through, she located and read some instances of its application. Still not understanding how it would help in her situation, she chose to disregard the instruction.

Judy obstinately endured more days of drudgery. The threatening and ever-present fear of the unknown led her into consistently darker nights.

Again, Judy felt the Holy Spirit speaking to her heart. She was to fast. Still questioning but desperately hopeful at this point, she finally succumbed to God's direction.

Her earthly thinking had exhausted its own understanding of what God was trying to prove to her; with an air nearly hinting of disregard, she made dinner and served the children only. She had long since allowed the return of eating in the family room, as it was far easier to dodge reality without the audience. Judy busied herself upstairs; she had returned to sorting the many piles of clothes she had begun addressing earlier.

Nighttime wore on, and once the children's dessert and bedtimes had passed, Judy had accomplished much. The clothing piles were reduced, and boxes that were labeled according to her original plans were becoming filled. Judy's empty stomach, however, was not. She retired for the night, hungry.

Another sleepless night loomed ahead. "This should be such a treat," uttered Judy sarcastically into the darkness. This night was proving to be deeper and darker than previous nights. She anxiously awaited the fingers of light to break through her window, driving the demons away into their hiding spots once more.

After lying restless for many hours, Judy turned the light on and tried to become absorbed in a book. After a long time of rereading sentences that were not registering in her weary mind, she decided to climb out of bed and get ready for work early.

After getting the children off to school, Judy pressed on into the morning. Her thoughts were scattered while doing her work. Kasey and her other coworkers, Jill and Brett, had voiced their concern that something was just not right. Judy didn't need to be told. She knew of her short temper, the shadows darkening her eyes, and now, as it was being noted, she was not eating. They were paying close attention.

"Judy, what is going on? We're worried. Maybe you should get help." Kasey stated firmly.

Judy stopped sorting the outgoing mail before her. She laid the envelopes down and turned to face her.

"I am fine. I know you guys care about me, and I thank you for that. I'm just going through a difficult time and need to be left alone for a while. I'm all right, really I am." Her stomach was growling loudly enough to be heard at this point.

Kasey looked her up and down with a frown. "Just know that we are here for you. You really should get something to eat." She reached out and touched Judy's arm tenderly then turned and walked back to Jill and Brett.

Judy chuckled inwardly. It was a magical laugh that had power. It seemed to crack the veil that had been draped over her. This was the first time light had broken through since Rich announced his infidelity in their bedroom. She was so hungry. Returning to her envelopes, turning her back on her staring coworkers, she resumed her sorting.

Her grumbling stomach led her to reach out to God, since he was the one who had requested this fast. *God, I am hungry! I won't question your will because I know you love me. I just ask for strength to follow your request.*

As her workday wore on, she found that God entered her mind more frequently. Each time the hunger pangs tugged at her, she thought of and talked to him.

That night Judy once again sent the kids to the family room with their plates to eat and watch TV. Though the kids seemed confused by Judy's change in attitude, they were very respectful of her by giving her the space and quiet time she needed. When the kids had asked about Rich's noted absence, she just couldn't face talking about it. What could she say? Not only was she struggling with his news; the added guilt at becoming distant and irritable with the kids once again was just too much to handle.

Judy returned to the clothing job upstairs. By the end of the night, she had completely sorted all that she had. She packed the clothes according to their destinations and put them in the car for distribution. She returned with dustpan and broom in hand to clean the hallway where, for many years, the clothes had occupied so much space.

Surveying the emptiness at the top of the stairs, she sought the connection with her Father once more. *Thank you for the energy and desire to complete this task in the face of such difficult times for me.*

It was time for bed. Lowering her head in defeat, as the negative thoughts were already taunting her,

Judy headed through her bedroom door to change her clothes. Her belly grumbled louder. *Okay, okay, Lord, I am so hungry! I am a weak person. It has only been just over a day, and I can't stop thinking about food. Let's change the subject. How was your day?* It humbled her once her own question sank in. How was *his* day?

Crawling into bed and shutting the light off, Judy continued her conversation. After a short time she began reciting the Lord's Prayer within her heart. She fell fast asleep before it was complete.

Two hours later Judy awoke, and the dark, sad thoughts began once more. But being awake also beckoned the pangs of hunger to return. *How is your night going? I'm hungry, no surprise.* Judy chuckled as her dark thoughts were replaced by a cheerful discussion with her Father. She envisioned Jesus standing beside her, holding her hand. She was so small compared to him, like a child holding hands with her parent. She smiled and snuggled deeper into her pillow, easily returning to sleep.

Around 4:30 a.m., Judy awoke with a consuming fear. Rich was going to fight for custody of the kids. She had been vicious for so long to them, and as a result of this behavior, the kids had misbehaved terribly. Surely the courts would see the correlation, and he would win them. Dread filled her as she envisioned herself a failure for all to see. Loneliness would surely plague her life as punishment. Strong hunger pangs returned, willing her to refocus her attention on God.

What should I do? Please, help me to let go and trust you!
The what-ifs are killing me! I need you; I need your peace.

Peace did then creep in, filling all the crevices of despair. But deeper still was the fasting revelation God had intended for her. This revelation would prove to be a great coping tool in difficult times. Turning from, or fasting from fear, from obsessive thinking, and refocusing on him anytime would allow peace to dispel darkness. Judy's trust in his power was renewed, and she was freed from the need to aimlessly grope for control.

Judy was happy as she clung to the image of Jesus holding her hand. Feeling completely protected, unbeatable, and excited for daylight in a new way, she drifted back to sleep to complete the most uplifting night she had enjoyed in some time.

chapter 10

It was the dawning of a new day in Judy's house. The weight of the past few weeks was lifted, and she felt lighter and younger as she danced down the stairs.

"Good morning." She greeted her children with a song in her voice, and they both looked up at her, befuddled.

Jamie had gotten used to being ignored lately and, with a raised eyebrow, scanned her mother's face. "Mom, are you okay?"

"I'm great; God is so good to me." She danced about the room.

"Mom…" Peter hesitated. "Mom, do you think I could have a friend over this weekend?"

Judy felt bad for the nervousness she could hear in her son's voice. She sensed the lack of security in their relationship. Her difficult time did have its negative effects on all of them. Judy was surprised but excited at his request. The kids never had friends over. The house was always such a mess that Judy, early on, had never allowed it.

Judy attempted to put Peter's mind at ease as she answered, "That would be great!" She saw the delighted response in his face. "In fact, since school is nearly out for the summer, why don't we call it an end-of-school party?" Turning to Jamie, Judy put her arm around her shoulders and continued, "You can both invite a bunch of friends. We can have music, a bonfire, and a cookout. Doesn't that sound fun?"

After quickly looking at each other, both kids turned and faced their mother; their mouths dropped open in exaggerated shock.

"Are you for real?" Jamie questioned.

"How many friends can I invite?" Peter asked, jumping right into the planning.

"I don't care; we have plenty of room. Each of you can choose one of your friends to stay overnight after the party now that your rooms are cleaned up too."

"Hooray!" Peter shouted as he jumped up and down.

"Today is Tuesday; hmm, let's plan it for Saturday from four o'clock until eight thirty. We'll bring your overnight friends home by eleven on Sunday morning." Judy wrote these times on the calendar so as not to forget.

The kids got ready for school with such excitement that they were ready early and had to wait. This had never happened before. It was amazing to Judy the impact God had; in affecting her, joy trickled down to the children as well.

While at work, Judy went into the office she shared with Kasey, John, Jill, and Brett. She held up the bagel in her hand and the cup of coffee, indicating her return to eating, and, with a smile on her face, sat down facing them.

"I want to share with you what has been going on so you can stop wondering and worrying. My husband left me a month ago. I've been struggling but have now come to terms with it."

They looked at her incredulously.

"What a jerk," Kasey muttered.

"I can't believe *he* left *you*. What's he got against nice people?" Brett responded.

"You don't deserve to be treated like that. Good riddance," John joined in.

Judy understood their negativity about Rich was intended to show support. She held up her hand. "Okay, guys, I appreciate your complaints, but I don't find them helpful. Rich is just doing what he feels he has to do. We haven't discussed what is happening next. I just wanted you to know since you were worried about me. Thanks for caring." With that, Judy got up and went to the sorting room to get to work.

While she was working, she felt the tug of direction that she had come to believe was God. After checking with her boss, Judy ducked out of work early and went to Haystacks to face reality.

Entering the store, she realized how much time had gone by since she had last been there. When Rich and Phil were starting the business, she had heard every detail and shared in the excitement. When they had first opened the store, she was frequently there, baby and dinner in tow. She had been a part of so much back then.

Their relationship deteriorated quite quickly once they were blessed with children. Judy had made them her focus, and Rich, she often pointed out, didn't know how to do anything right. He became a workaholic, diving deeply into making the store a success. That was his baby.

She looked around at the walls and the partitioned areas. There were sections dedicated to farming, gardening, and pets. There were items for tapping trees, brewing beer, and feeding wild birds. Things had changed so much as the store had evolved to better match the needs of its customers. A pang of sadness touched her heart as she realized this was not a part of her anymore.

Courtney, a young mother of two, looked up from her post behind the counter and smiled warmly. "Hi, Judy, how have you been? I haven't seen you in here in a long time."

She seemed so innocent and sweet, and a question hit Judy's gut. *Could this be the one?*

"Hi, Courtney. I'm fine. Is Rich around?" The butterflies in her stomach were multiplying by the second. She knew she had to refocus and began to silently pray for strength.

"He's in his office; go ahead back."

"Thanks." How distant and removed from Rich's life Judy felt. Passing Courtney, she stepped around the counter and headed down the hallway to the offices.

chapter 11

Rich was in his office on the phone placing an order when he saw Judy step into the doorway. She raised her hand in a light greeting. He felt nervousness grip his insides as he waved her in. He wrapped up the call and replaced the phone in its cradle. "Hi, Judy." He watched her as she closed the door and sat in one of the two overstuffed chairs facing his desk. "How have you been?"

Judy looked up at him but was slow to answer. "Fine. We need to talk." Intentional or not, it didn't escape him that his own words from a month ago were being repeated.

"I'm sorry I haven't called. I have been very confused. I guess I've been afraid to face what I've done and what that means for all of us." Rich had rehearsed this moment time and time again but yet could still not find the right words. How could he face her after what he had done? His heart was heavy, and the weight of the guilt was enormous.

"That makes two of us," Judy responded.

"How are the kids?" Rich sheepishly inquired.

"Fine. I haven't told them anything about you leaving yet."

"Why not?" Rich asked, surprised.

"I had to go through my own feelings before I could face talking to them. Besides, I really don't know what's going on yet. That's why I'm here."

Years earlier a discussion such as this would never have taken place. Talking was never an option. She would argue, and he would resign.

Rich remembered the years of his infidelity before Judy's changes. He hadn't looked for it, planned it, or even wished it. It had just happened.

There were many nights when the store closed that he couldn't stand the thought of going home. Aggression always filled the air of their house. It was such an uncomfortable feeling that delaying it was not just a wish but a necessity.

It was a night such as this that he went to the diner to eat a late dinner. He hadn't been to this particular restaurant often. Sitting alone on the barstool, he ordered a cheeseburger, fries, and water and waited in quiet contemplation for their arrival. He thought of work and the pressures he felt there, though the business was going well. He thought of the kids and how much they had grown, how much he didn't really know them at all. He thought of Judy and how he didn't care to know her. That made him sad. He felt as though he had been wasting years away, stuck in a bad marriage.

"Hey, you seem deep in thought. Is everything okay?"

Rich looked up at her. She was pretty: blonde, blue eyes, and slender. "Just a lot on my mind, I guess."

"Anything you want to talk about? I'm a good listener." Crystal, the waitress, leaned on the counter, turning an ear toward Rich as if to point out that fact to him.

"I don't know. Why does life have to be so messy?" Rich shook his head in frustration.

"Messy? What do you mean?" She watched Rich, who remained quiet for a minute. She encouraged him to share his frustrations. "Come on. Lay it out and let's take a look."

"I think I'm a great guy. I work hard and provide for my family, but all I get are complaints. My wife always feels she has to point out my failures. I'm at the point of giving up."

Rich continued with his plight as Crystal listened. They took an occasional break as Crystal tended to the last few customers she had. Rich took advantage of these moments to devour his meal.

It felt so good to have someone to talk to who didn't seem to have an agenda. Crystal, unlike Judy, did not judge every word spoken in search of a fight;

she just listened. Rich hung longer at the diner, enjoying the company of his newfound friend.

When finally it was time to head home, Rich felt invigorated and encouraged. It had helped so much to share his burden and "lay it out," as Crystal had suggested. He felt much better. He had entered his house that night quite a bit later than usual and, of course, was faced with an irate wife. She didn't seem to care that he was late really; she just loved to attack and appeared happy for the excuse.

"You don't even care enough to call so I can plan dinnertime accordingly. How disrespectful can you get anyway?" The screaming continued, and the encouragement he had felt on the way home slipped into the fog of his mind as he tried to block the attacks.

Eventually, going to the diner for late dinners became regular. Judy stopped cooking for him altogether as a punishment for his not caring, and Crystal became Rich's counselor of sorts. She never did open up and discuss her home life. She remained a listener. The conversations were focused on Rich.

The kind listening became kind hugs, which led to an intimacy neither should have entertained. The boundary was breeched and therefore was never clear again. Both were married, and both remained secrets. The encouragement turned to forbidden excitement that led to guilty necessity. It was a game they never should have played but became too enmeshed in to stop.

He had spent so much time justifying this affair to himself. He had been so mistreated by Judy. In a way, he felt as though he had the upper hand. He was winning every fight, could gloat inwardly, and she never even knew it.

It was years into this affair when Judy had her spiritual awakening. Rich watched his wife transform from an angry and irrational beast into a beautiful and peaceful angel. The guilt compounded, and the distance Judy was trying to bridge became terrifying to him.

Judy no longer fought with Rich. She showed a love he had never known, even when their relationship was young. Over time, Judy chose to stop complaining and was positive about nearly everything. The beauty within melded with her outward attractiveness. She was gorgeous. He would find himself watching her, but knowing the dark secrets he hid, he could not reach out to her.

Instead of discreetly winning a battle against his wife, he had successfully ended the chance of a great life with his own family. The shame shot deep within his heart. The greater life was at home, the deeper the hurt was within him, and the more he remained silent and separate. He now realized he did not deserve her.

Rich focused on Judy's face once more, pushing the thoughts of his infidelity aside. He knew what he had done was terrible. He knew he could never make it up to her.

chapter 12

"Rich, what is going on? You haven't called or come back. I'm assuming you don't need anything from the house." Judy appeared uncomfortable as she spoke.

"We closed on the loan for our second store in Amesbury. There is an apartment above it, and I've been staying there. I'm going to be sending you money to help with the kids. I'd like to start having them come to visit me. You'll have to tell them that we've split up."

"Okay." Judy looked at her hands briefly, as if deep in thought, then continued. "I can bring them over on Sunday, perhaps around lunchtime? Is that good for you? They are having friends over for an end-of-school-year party Saturday, and the kids staying over-night will be going home just before noon."

Rich furrowed his eyebrows; a quizzical look crossed his face. "You are letting the kids have a party at the house?"

"Peter asked, and since the house is getting straightened around, I agreed." Looking down again, Judy continued quietly, "I'm sorry for having you guys live in all that mess for so long." Judy paused as a look of sadness came to her beautiful features. "I have gotten rid of all the clothes and have tried to keep up with the cleaning. What a bad habit I have been in. It wasn't fair to you guys." A tear slipped free and slid down her cheek.

Rich looked at her and felt a tug at his heart. He wanted so much to wipe the tear away and hold her. How could he have thrown away his rights to comfort his own wife? A glance at the clock on the wall above Judy reminded Rich he had to leave. The timing was terrible.

"Well, I'm glad they're getting this opportunity." Sounding a bit harsher then he had intended, Rich continued, "I'm sorry, but I have to get to the other store. I have a three o'clock meeting with a vendor, and I hadn't realized how late it was getting."

Judy rose, appearing embarrassed, and wiped the wet tear from her cheek. Rich handed her a business card and pointed out the address of the new store. Their fingers touched briefly. Rich felt a tingle, a tug at his heart, followed by a desire for a love he no longer deserved.

Judy quickly filled the awkward space with a suggestion as she placed his business card in her pocket. "I'll call your cell Sunday when we're on our way."

"That sounds good, and I'll have them home by seven thirty so they can settle in for bedtime." Rich walked to the door with Judy.

"Thank you." Judy stepped to the hallway and looked back at her husband. "I am sorry for how badly I treated you. I'm sorry that I pushed you away. I do hope you are happy now." Her words sounded completely sincere and held not a trace of malice. Judy quickly turned and walked past Courtney and out the front door.

Rich closed the office door, sat in the seat his wife had just vacated, and wept. *Sorry? Sorry? How could she feel sorry?* He had done her wrong. He wasn't happy now. What was she thinking? He wanted his family. He wanted the wife he had watched from a distance for nearly a year. He wanted to share the joy of raising their children together.

His wife, with all the love she could muster, wished him happiness. The pain was searing. The grief was overwhelming. She was such a wonderful person now. Why had he given in to lust? What a hypocrite he had been, angrily judging his wife for her mistreatment only to return evil for evil. He didn't believe in getting back at people. That was not who he was. It did not represent his beliefs. He sobbed until he was empty and then rose from the chair. Grabbing his keys, he slipped out the back door to his car and drove to attend to business, submersing himself in work yet again to avoid the pain of his personal life.

Yes, he had justified this affair by blaming Judy originally, but over the last eight months, Rich had struggled greatly with the position he had gotten himself into. He knew it was wrong. He knew he would have to pay a consequence. As the confusion grew in his head, denial became his protection. Outside of lessening his visits to Crystal, he didn't do anything differently. He couldn't face his wife or the truth of what he was doing. He was trying to put the inevitable as far away as possible.

The truth will set you free. This statement had kept filling his mind. For weeks before he confessed to Judy, it haunted him. *The truth will set you free.* There was no logic to it. The truth would bring consequence. The truth would take his wife, his home, and his children. It would negatively affect his business. The truth would cause him to lose all he had. It could not possibly bring freedom.

Ironically though, exposing the truth had done just that. He was now free. No longer was he fearful of the day his sin was to be exposed, because now it was. No longer did he desire to quench the lust he frequently held in secret, because he no longer felt it. By speaking the truth, the spell of lusty desire was broken. The secret that held power became powerless. He was starting over, but he was free to begin living right.

He had told Crystal that he couldn't continue their affair. He shared with her the confession to his wife and that, through facing what they had been doing all these years, he realized he was terribly wrong. He needed to end the inappropriate behavior.

Though it was Crystal's understanding that led him into danger originally, he was glad for it now.

chapter 13

Judy drove away feeling sad but uplifted. Facing the inevitable had been necessary. She could feel the spirit within and that she was surrounded by God's grace. She knew that she would love her husband no matter what was to happen, no matter what he'd done, because that was the love God had given to her. It was unconditional.

Now she was going to meet the children at the bus stop, take them to the store for treats, and settle down to a discussion of facts. Life had changed, for all of them.

The kids tumbled off the bus giggling. They were so excited about their upcoming party, and they had eagerly spread the word to all. Judy was not quite sure what she had gotten herself into. They climbed into the car, each talking over the other, sharing their friends' names and the plans of what they hoped to do at the party. So much busyness caught Judy off guard.

She suddenly wondered if she would be able to handle a houseful of rambunctious kids.

As she drove to the store, she let the kids' excitement flow. Grinning frequently into the rearview mirror, she was thrilled by their expressions. She hoped that their excitement wouldn't be destroyed by what she had to share with them next.

After a short drive, Judy parked and got out of the car. "Everybody out," Judy exclaimed as she opened the back door of her Subaru, ushering the kids to the door of their local convenience store.

Jamie stopped at the door and looked back at her mother. "What's going on?"

"I just thought we could get a treat. Grab a drink and some chips or a candy bar, whatever you want," Judy answered, not ready to expose the ulterior motive that brought them here just yet. Peter did not question. He tugged the door open and bolted through.

Judy partially filled a large cup with ice and doused it with iced tea, filling the cup to its rim. After placing bubble covers on two smaller cups, Judy handed them to her kids to fill as they desired from the slushy machine. Jamie chose to fill her cup with the taste of green apple, topping it off with a touch of red watermelon. Peter played the slushy field and layered each of the four flavors repeatedly until the top of the cover was reached. Judy slid a straw into the frosty mixture so he could take his first sip. After some time browsing the options of snacks, each of the kids opted for candy bars to complete their rare but sweet treat. Judy paid the cashier and helped the two back into the car. Before opening her own door, she raised her head a bit to the heavens and uttered a short prayer under her breath as the butterflies fluttered around her stomach. It was time.

Having decided earlier that home was not the place to broach the subject, Judy drove to the boat access at Mirror Lake and parked the car. The kids, now very suspicious, asked what was going on.

"Let's sit to sort of a picnic, a sugary snack picnic. I need to talk with you guys, and I thought this would be a good place to do it." Judy opened her door and got out then opened their door for them since their hands were full.

The kids went to the water's edge; Judy went to the picnic table off to the left of the sandy beach and sat down. She watched as her kids chatted together, looking out over the water. Putting their drinks down, they both opened their candy bars and bit into them. It was cute how they seemed to so often mimic one another, no competition between them present anymore. It wasn't clear whether one followed the other or if they merely followed through on similar thoughts at the same time.

They were getting along so well now, Peter and Jamie. She hoped that the changes she was ready to announce would not thwart the growth they had achieved. Their relationship with each other was special, school was going well, their home life was comfortable, and life had reached a fine balance for them. Were they ready for such a major change?

Judy thought on the upcoming visitation Rich was requesting with the kids. This was such a strange prospect, and truthfully, she wasn't sure how she felt about it. It had never really struck her before that Rich never had spent any time alone with the kids. She had not worried in a long time about Rich's parenting. It now dawned on her that it was because he really hadn't been involved. Now he would have them, one-on-one, without her. Even though she knew this was good for them, the adjustment of it might be quite trying for all.

This also meant that she was now going to be alone without her kids. She had not had time to ponder on that much either. Her heart fell just a bit. She couldn't imagine that time alone. She could foresee the mourning she would endure. It was as if tragedy had not yet occurred but she knew it was coming.

There will be good coming from this, God assured Judy. He would carry her through. She needed to let go of each of their situations. Each of them would confront, endure, and transform as he intended. They each, as individuals, needed what lay ahead.

Taking a deep breath, ready to face the inevitable, she pulled herself out of her own thinking and returned her attention to the kids.

"Hey, guys, come over here," Judy beckoned to them, gesturing for them to sit on the picnic bench opposite her.

chapter 14

Crossing the boat launch, Peter and Jamie slowly walked in Judy's direction, sipping their slushies as they continued talking to each other about the party.

"Have a seat; I want to go over some things with you."

"We will be good, Mom. Don't worry." Peter sounded a bit concerned.

Tears threatened Judy's eyes instantly in reaction. "What do you mean, you will be good?" Judy asked.

Jamie jumped in quickly. "Me, Peter, our friends, we'll be good. Don't worry so much. You'll have fun too!"

Judy realized they were talking about the party. She shook her head and smiled at her own confusion. Now she chuckled at the thought of joining the fun of her kids and their friends. That wasn't a picture she had envisioned before. "I'm sure everything will be fine with your friends. I'm glad you're so excited. You're right, though, I am a bit worried. There will be a lot of fooling around, and I'm not sure how I'll handle it."

"Why did you buy us the treats then? And why are we here if it wasn't about the party?" Peter asked.

"What do you need to tell us?" Jamie sounded concerned.

Taking a deep breath, Judy spoke softly. "Kids, Dad and I have split up."

The intake of breath by the both of them was audible. They looked at each other incredulously.

Jamie spoke first. "Why didn't you tell us?" She looked away in confusion. "I even asked you about him. You told me he was busy at work."

Peter listened quietly but was looking down at his lap. He raised his head but not his eyes. "Our family was always the different one. Everyone else's parents are divorced." He took a slow, deep breath. "I liked that about us."

Judy felt his pain but continued. "Haystacks just opened another store in Amesbury, and Dad is staying in an apartment above it."

"A new store…" Jamie pondered briefly. "Maybe he has so much work to do at the new store that he has to stay there?" There was hope in Jamie's voice.

Judy had spent time in her own denial and understood it well, but she reconfirmed the point to her daughter. "No, we have split up. He is busy, but that is not why—"

"What happened?" Peter interrupted in a quiet but firm voice. He was no longer excited and happy looking but confused and withdrawn.

"Guys, look, we both love you very much."

Peter slumped where he sat. "No, he doesn't. He doesn't even care about us. He's never around."

Judy turned to focus on Peter. "He does love you; he loves you both very much. His leaving had nothing to do with either of you. He left because of problems between the two of us."

Jamie's response was far too curt. "He's a jerk. I don't care that he's gone. It'll be better without him."

"Your father is not a jerk!" Judy's reaction was immediate and strong. It surprised even herself under the circumstances. She was very concerned with her children's differing reactions. "He may not have been very involved with you guys, but that was not his fault; it was mine."

"You didn't do anything wrong, Mom; Dad just loved work more." Peter was still quiet in his interjections.

Swallowing hard, Judy continued in her support of her husband. "Peter, since you were born I took over all of the parenting. I spent many years correcting your father when I should have just let him be a dad. I was wrong. Your father had to put up with a lot because of me. After years of me constantly nagging him, he just had enough. I don't blame him."

Peter's sweet voice corrected Judy. "Mom, you don't nag at Dad."

"Honey, I've changed a lot. God has been working on me and will continue to, but I did nag at Daddy all the time before. I'm sure you remember all the screaming I used to do. Daddy didn't appreciate it, nor did he deserve it."

Jamie pulled her frame up, straightened her back, took another sip of her slushy, and, with piercing eyes, looked at her mother. "You were mean. I remember how mean you were to him, and to us too, all the time." Her eyes were reduced to slits showing her anger.

Though sad, Judy took all her kids' confusion and anger in, just enough to piece together her role of supporter and encourager. It was good that all this was finally being talked about. They needed to talk about the past. They also needed to face the present and be ready for the future, open for whatever it was going to offer.

"Yes, I was mean, I remember. I remember when God opened my eyes and showed me how awful I was being. It made me sick inside. It hurt me in a way I had never felt before, realizing how much I was hurting all of you." Jamie turned her back and faced the water. "Looking back, I don't understand how I thought I had the right to bully everyone around. As I said, God opened my eyes. He forgave me and offered me guidance. He made me into someone new. Though I have struggled over our breakup, God has encouraged me and given me peace, which gets me through difficult times. I want you to understand he is here for you both as well. This may be difficult for all of us, but we can trust him." Taking a deep, shuddered breath, Judy finished, "I love you both." At these words Jamie turned back around but wouldn't look at her mother.

Peter looked back to his mother and asked, "Mom, are you mad at Dad?"

"No, Peter. I was hurt and scared, and I guess I did go through a short time of being mad. You guys saw that, and I'm sorry." Judy took a moment to look at the face of each child. "He told me he was leaving quite a few weeks ago. I didn't share it with you until I could face it myself. I love him and miss him, but I do support and respect his decision."

"Maybe he would come back home if you told him that. I mean, if he knows that you love him, he would be happy, right?"

Judy reached out and touched Peter's hand. "No, honey. I think right now Daddy needs his space." She continued, "Sunday, after we take the last of your friends home, I'm taking you both to Dad's new place. He will bring you back after dinner. He wants to spend some time with you."

Jamie stood abruptly at this news and turned her back once more on her mother. "He's gonna ruin my life!" With that she stormed off and got back in the car, leaving her drink and empty candy wrapper behind.

Peter watched his sister leave the table. Judy sat with him in silence for a time. She was letting each of them confront the situation however they needed. It seemed as though Jamie would rebel and Peter would withdraw. Judy was hopeful for better, though.

chapter 15

By the time Saturday had arrived, Judy was beside herself with frustration. Peter was overly compassionate toward his mother for the loss of her marriage; Jamie, on the other hand, was furious at the consequences they were all surely going to pay due to her mother's past bullying.

Their opinions and subsequent reactions differed greatly, but neither of them gave mention to what this would mean to their own relationship with their father. The realization that ever since their children were young Judy had undermined and effectively erased Rich's parental relationship with his children now became sadly obvious to her.

She had spent the past few nights encouraging Peter to not worry about her and, at the same time, trying to get Jamie to not be so hateful toward her. She also tried to encourage a relationship between them and their father, though neither seemed to buy into this discussion. Both seemed uncomfortable about the subject of their dad and didn't want to talk about it.

The end-of-school party was to begin in just an hour, and Judy was trying to pull together the condiments and paper supplies needed for the barbecue. She had the wood stacked and ready for the bonfire, had the S'more fixings together in a plastic bin, ready to pull out at the appointed time, and had cried a bit in the bathroom to release the anxiety she had pent up.

The first child, a friend of Peter's, arrived half an hour early, catching Judy completely by surprise. By ten after four, sixteen additional kids, nine of Jamie's friends and seven of Peter's, had filled the yard. Thankfully, Jamie and Peter had clear ideas of what they wanted to accomplish during this party and had quickly organized a game of tag. Judy did not have to entertain.

Free to make dinner, she shaped the patties, opened the hot dog packages, and brought them all to the table she had set up beside the grill. She and Rich had bought this grill on sale at the end of last season. She was thankful now that they had bought big. Surely she needed the extra grill space tonight.

While grilling the burgers, she had time to relax and watch all the kids running around. They were laughing and completely enjoying themselves. Seeing her kids interact with their friends was so endearing. It was also nice to see Jamie smiling again. Of course, that smile disappeared as soon as she caught sight of her mother looking in her direction.

As each dog and burger finished cooking, Judy added them to the table where the potato salad, soda, chips, condiments, plates, napkins, and cups were. They vanished nearly as fast as she took them off the grill. Judy kept up the grilling until the last dogs and burgers were charred sufficiently. Grabbing a cheese-burger before they were all gone, she enjoyed her meal alone feeling a sense of great accomplishment.

The kids had moved on to hide and seek as the darkness of night enveloped the group. Judy, Girl Scout skills still intact, built a fire even the coldest dog-sledder from Antarctica could appreciate. Though the night was warm, the fire's glow and the call of marsh-mallows beckoned nearly the whole crowd. It was a good thing Judy had cut so many sprigs to roast the marshmallows on.

As most of the kids settled around the fire and it was getting close to the end of the party, Judy real-ized Jamie was no longer in their midst. She wan-dered around the few stragglers at the outskirts of the fire's shine but did not see her there either. She walked through the house and, reaching the top step, heard her daughter's voice as she was chatting with Stephanie, her friend that was to stay overnight.

"What if Mom can't afford us living here anymore, and what will I do if she can't pay for me to dance next year? I can't quit; I love it. Dancing is my life!"

"Yeah, things will change. My parents divorced when I was little. Just imagine, though, you'll get two

Christmases, two Easters, two birthdays; that's not so bad."

"She screwed up, and now I'm gonna have to give up the things I want? No way!"

Judy was shocked and instantly irritated at the selfishness of her daughter. She took a step down, suddenly uncomfortable that she was eavesdropping. She returned to the crowd outside with her daughter's questions now settling deeper in her mind.

Rich had said he was going to send money to help support the kids, but would supporting two lifestyles be too much for them both? Where would they go if they couldn't stay here? Even though they had gotten a great deal on their house, their mortgage payments were quite high. It had been affordable when their incomes were pooled, but what now?

She also felt sad that her now fourteen-year-old daughter was concerning herself with adult financial worries, issues Judy had always sheltered her from in the past. Light was now being shed on the anger Jamie had been expressing toward her mother. A sense of direction was being presented; Judy only needed guidance and wisdom to lead her daughter ahead.

Parents began arriving to pick up their children. Judy found it difficult to visit with them with so many thoughts and ideas mulling through her head. They seemed to want to chat, a general attempt at social connection. Judy's answers were short, and her attention was disconnected.

"Yes, it was a great night." "Yes, they seemed to have a lot of fun." "He fell but only got a scratch, nothing serious." "Yes, your daughter was very polite." "No, I didn't realize he had thrown up last night." *Wish I'd known that one before now.*

The formalities and pleasantries were driving her mad at this point. She just wanted to settle into bed and seek God's direction for her own children.

Soon the party was only present in memory, except for the few plates and cups strewn about the lawn. The two kids with their overnight friends were off in their respective bedrooms chatting about Pokémon, body changes, bodily gasses, and divorce. Judy sat watching the embers of the fire brighten and change; small flames licked all around them, dancing and reducing them in short time to mere ash. That was just about how Judy felt. Change was licking around her, reducing all that she knew to something not quite recognizable anymore. Her very being and all she thought that mattered in her life was threatening to change. She doused the last glowing embers with the hose and watched the brightness become engulfed in smoke; the sudden hissing quickly became faint.

The burning of the dross. Judy sat in the dark warmth of the night, these words laid upon her heart. The burning of the dross—she remembered reading about this, and now, with the fire having finished its job of transforming the wood to brittle ash, she thought on its meaning as it must pertain to her life. To ensure a metal is pure, it is melted at such a high heat that any impurities are burned out. She vaguely remembered having read a comparison of this to a believer's life in the Bible. Suddenly Judy had an awakening, a revelation, as to its pertinence to her very circumstances.

With elation she thought through this scenario: Since she had placed God first and foremost, at the center of her life, he was now bringing about all that was necessary for her spiritual peace and prosperity. He was allowing circumstances meant to remove impurities from her life, and what directly affected her would also affect those she loved, for the better. Whatever was to become of them financially was going to be just fine, for it was all part of his plan. Hope overflowed anew, and peace, once again, resumed its position within her soul.

After cleaning up the table and the yard, Judy went inside. Poking her head into each of the kids' rooms, she smiled and wished them all a good night. She was so much less concerned about what could be, for she was now sure of what was. She retired to the sanctuary of her bedroom and changed into her pajamas. After brushing her teeth she crawled into bed and, though she in no way knew what lay ahead, began thanking God for all He had done, for both the good and the bad.

chapter 16

Judy called Rich to alert him they were on their way. The children all piled into the car, and Judy felt oddly excited that she was going to have the afternoon to herself. As the deliveries of friends to their homes were made and the direction of travel became focused on Amesbury, the chatter in the backseat ceased. Judy's attention was drawn to the faces in her rearview mirror, each staring blankly out their separate windows.

"I hope you have an awesome afternoon," Judy said cheerfully.

She caught a glance at their astonished faces in the rearview mirror as the children turned to look at the back of Judy's head.

"I don't want to go," Peter mumbled quietly.

Jamie merely turned, after loudly expelling a breath, back to glare out the window.

"I think Dad is really excited about this time with you. This is a great opportunity for you to have the relationships you've not really had." Judy's voice was drippy with hope and encouragement. "Everything will be fine. Consider this a chance to start over. See what God has in store for you."

Apparently this was too much sweetness for Jamie, as she retorted, "We wouldn't be going through this if it wasn't for you."

Peter was mad. "Cut it out! Stop being mean to Mom!" He turned to look out his window, and a tear slid down his cheek.

Emotions were high for her children. "Change is difficult to face, guys," Judy offered in condolence. But face it they must. Judy was not uncomfortable about this anymore. She also chose to no longer carry the burden of each of their experiences on her shoulders. She was not in control, God was, and she gladly embraced this fact. Her children would endure, embracing or rebelling, each lesson God led them through. Though this might prove unbearable at times, she was willing to let them be, guided by the hands of her Lord.

The ride was long and quiet. They arrived at Rich's home within forty-five minutes.

"Here we are." Judy got out and led the children to the apartment door, holding it open as the kids hesitantly passed her and ascended the stairwell before them. Rich opened the door at the top and happily greeted his family.

"Hi, guys! How are you?" Hearing no response, he quickly continued, "Welcome to my home away from home." Rich stepped back and ushered all in to his large apartment. It filled the entire top floor of Haystacks Feed and Grain. Windows let in light from every direction. As the kids wandered through the sparsely furnished apartment, Judy and Rich stood together.

Ignoring the tug of jealousy and the sadness as the tangible proof of their separate lives lay before her, Judy said, "This is very nice, Rich. If there is anything you need from the house, please feel free to let me know." As the kids wandered into adjoining rooms to check out the place, Judy whispered, "They are struggling with this, but I think it will be good for them, and for you too. I told them this is their chance to start over again with you, to create relationships I never could seem to allow you to have."

Rich turned to look at Judy, absorbing her words as the kids, now filled with excitement, joined them in the kitchen.

Judy smiled at her children as she spoke. "Have fun, kids. I'll see you tonight." She kissed Peter and waved to Jamie, who was avoiding any affection from her; then Judy opened the door and headed down the stairs.

Rich followed, stopping her with his words. "Thanks. For bringing the kids, I mean. Here's a check for you." He stepped down and handed it to her.

"Thank you." Taking the check, Judy looked back up at Rich. "There is a lot we have to consider, you know."

They were avoiding talking, avoiding making decisions, avoiding the damage of hurtful behaviors. They had to face the changes, overwhelming as they were.

Judy continued, "We really need to get together to talk about it all."

"You're right. We should come up with a visitation schedule and talk about the finances and legal paperwork," Rich suggested.

"Okay, just let me know when, and I'll try to get some time off from work. It might be best during the day when the kids aren't around. They don't need to hear any of what we have to discuss." Judy felt her strength wavering as she stood in the stairwell.

"That makes sense. I'll let you know." Rich returned to the top of the stairs. "I'll see you later."

"Okay, have fun." Judy watched the door close and heard the excited commotion as Rich joined their children. After leaving the building, she sat in her car looking up at the windows of her husband's home. *Her husband's home.* It sounded odd but felt, at this moment, so right. She glanced down at the check in her hand. Her heart jumped at the numbers before her. It was written for fourteen hundred dollars. On the memo line he had scrawled the words, "Child Support." How concrete that sounded.

"Okay, Judith, let's move on." Chuckling at the words that had just escaped her lips, she put the car in reverse and did just that, moved on.

She went to lunch alone, ordering chicken Parmesan and a side salad, and thoroughly enjoyed the complimentary warm roll. After dining, she wandered the shops in town, acknowledging the need for a hobby, something to fill her alone time, not as a distraction but as enrichment and enjoyment. Her time alone was not to be a punishment, no matter how much Jamie would wish this on her. She would embrace it as a gift from God and was open to do whatever he willed. He, in return, offered her freedom and the assurance that whatever she chose to do he would bless.

Judy settled on oil painting. She was artistic by nature and had spent years as a child doodling and creating wonderful pencil sketches. Now, standing in the craft store before the display of paint, brushes, easels, and canvases, she felt excited. After gathering the supplies she thought she might need, she headed to the checkout.

Driving home she imagined the beautiful scenes she could bring to life. With a bit of practice, patience, and determination, she believed the images she cherished could be beckoned from her mind and made a reality on canvas.

She had to find a spot to set up at the house, an artist's retreat of sorts. Wandering through each room in her mind proved to be ineffective. She realized that she would need to wait, to physically enter each room, each corner, each nook. She needed to stand in and feel every available space. The right area would call to her; she would know.

After pulling into the drive, she left all her supplies in the car, running excitedly in the door to search for a location. Browsing each room, she stopped on occasion to see if the vision of an art studio felt right or not. She would look from every direction, knowing that sometimes the right thing is not so obvious. She wandered upstairs as well, open to all possibilities.

When her hunt was complete, she returned to the car to retrieve her supplies. She was so excited. In two trips, she had laid all she had bought at the prospective site, ready to arrange and conform.

After two hours of moving furniture and arranging and rearranging art supplies and tools, the task was accomplished. She stood back at the doorway to look at all she had changed in her bedroom, her new sanctuary. It had taken on a completely different feel as she gazed over the changes she had incorporated. No longer would this space support division; it would now support creation and life. It would be a party to the making of visions and hopes and beauty. Passion would fill the walls of this refuge in a new way.

Sinking into the loveseat, now facing the studio area, she smiled. The feeling, the atmosphere of the room as a whole, took on a new meaning. *Retreat—* this word only touched the depth of what she believed it would be for her. However, she wanted to share its peace with her children as well. Hopefully, as she had set the room up, it would prove inviting and welcoming to them whenever they so desired to merely visit or perhaps join her in creating.

It was now getting past dinnertime. Having been so wrapped up in her project, Judy had failed to acknowledge the growling of her stomach. She reheated some leftovers, turned the news on, and eagerly awaited the greeting of her children.

Rich's car pulled in the yard, and the side door opened. Her husband soon filled the doorway of the kitchen. It felt weird to have him in this space now. Jamie went directly to her room, avoiding her mother still. Peter brushed past his father and came to plant a big, wet kiss on Judy's cheek.

"Hi, Mom," Peter said as he draped his arms about his mother's neck, a bit louder and more clingy than usual.

Turning to look into his sweet face, Judy answered suspiciously, "Hi, Peter. How was your day?" She was hoping this overly affectionate act wasn't a play against his father. It was understandable that he would feel a bit different under the circumstances.

Releasing the hold on his mother, Peter turned to hang on the refrigerator door instead. As he pulled it open, he responded, "We had a great time! We went to the movies, and Dad let me have popcorn, soda, *and* a candy bar." His words were becoming muffled, as he was now rummaging deep in the fridge.

Judy timidly smiled at Rich as she continued her conversation with Peter. "What are you looking for?"

"I'm hungry. Isn't it dessert time?" He pulled his head out of the fridge, with yogurt, chocolate sauce, and Cool Whip balancing in his arms.

Judy laughed. "You just listed all the junk food you had. How hungry can you be?"

Peter began to protest when Rich interrupted, "The movie was at one. They did have a good dinner at five, but because we've been out, we didn't have dessert yet. I'm sorry."

Judy rose to join Rich in the entryway, affectionately rustling Peter's hair as she passed by him. "No, don't be. I don't mind."

Rich retreated to the door. Opening it to go, he turned to face his wife. "I would like to get together this week if you can. Call me with a good time." Rich stopped for a moment then continued. "I realized very quickly that I didn't know my own kids once we were alone. It was awkward. I would like to change that, the sooner the better. Peter is so shy around me, and Jamie is growing up fast. I can't believe I missed so much. I'd like us to work together to create a good schedule for all of us."

Rich smiled. He seemed to feel comfortable sharing these feelings with Judy. That was something that would not have taken place in the past.

Kindly, Judy acknowledged the same hope. "I know it sounds weird, but I do believe everything is for a reason—a higher purpose, I suppose. You guys need this time to create relationships you rightfully should have had all along."

"Judy, I don't deserve this time." Looking away as if in shame, Rich continued, "I'm available to talk anytime this week. Give me a call." He quickly stepped out, closing the door behind him.

Judy stood at the closed door regaining her composure. She was confused by his statement. *He is a good man. These are his children. Of course he deserves this time with them.* Shaking her head, she returned to the kitchen to visit with Peter.

chapter 17

Their meeting took place in Rich's office at Haystacks, where they had met and talked briefly a week before. Judy had gotten out of work shortly after lunchtime, which allotted them approximately two hours to accomplish much of what was on their minds.

Being greeted by Courtney at the counter as she passed through, Judy suppressed the urge to flee. The question arose in her heart, once again, of who Rich's mistress was. Taking a deep breath and uttering a quick prayer for strength to top off the past three hours of continuous discussion with God, Judy opened her hands, symbolically laying her jealousy at the foot of the cross. Rich was in God's hands too. Judy had to focus first and foremost on God, not fix or change anyone else. She quickly reminded herself of this as she knocked on the closed office door.

Expecting to hear him call for her to come in, she was surprised when he opened the door for her. Rich ushered her in and back to the same seat she had sat in before. He, on the other hand, did not return to the other side of his desk but chose to sit in the chair beside her, having turned the seats to subtly face one another with a coffee table set to the side.

"Hi, Judy. Thanks for taking time off of work to come." His words were so formal.

Judy looked at the table before them, which was laden with legal papers. A rush of fear gripped her as the sense of finality snaked around the room. Had she expected this to all disappear and life to return to normal? She supposed not; normal for them had not been good. She had wished for a chance to make their marriage healthy, but here they were, divorce papers at their sides. The relationship with the other woman must have been strong if he was so set on divorce.

Rich was watching Judy's face and asked with concern, "Are you okay?" Her struggle must have been obvious.

"Of course, I'm fine," she answered as she sat in her seat.

He pointed to the documents as he also sat down. "These are the papers we are supposed to file with the courts to begin the process."

The process…the process…oh, just say it. Divorce! Her heart sank. Had the denial been so strong for her that she had felt there would be no sadness? This was suddenly a "walk by faith" moment, and peace was a struggle.

"Phil had a divorce a couple of years ago. It was terrible; their lawyers had them fighting over everything, including their kids," Rich explained about his business partner.

Judy was surprised. She had known Phil and Stacy when they met, married, and had their three kids. She didn't even know they were having problems, let alone that they had divorced two years ago. She and Rich really had not been close. Much had happened in her husband's life that he hadn't shared. It was clear they had no friendship in their marriage. Surely it was best that what little they had should end.

"I don't want this to be bad for us or the kids, so I gathered all the information needed to file for an uncontested divorce. Uncontested means without a fight and that we agree on the terms of the divorce as *we* outline them, not lawyers. I thought we could go through the papers together to see if you feel the same." Rich sounded so businesslike, so impersonal.

"I don't want to fight over stuff, certainly not over our children," Judy responded in a stupor.

"I want to be sure your needs are met and the kids don't suffer any unjust consequences," Rich offered assuringly.

There would be consequences, both good and bad. Difficult as this was, all was happening for a reason. Judy did not want the children to suffer either and felt confident the best would come for them. Two peaceful homes, healthy relationships with each of their parents, these were things they had not had up until now.

With trembling hand, she took the first paper Rich handed to her. He held a copy as well and began, line by line, explaining what was needed. Document by document, Rich continued. The end of them as a couple was tangible, and it felt awful.

Once he finished explaining the forms, he asked quite kindly, "Are you comfortable filling these out together? I assumed you wouldn't want a lawyer, but perhaps you do."

"No, this is fine." What was she saying? How was she supposed to feel? His mention of lawyers caused her to think of the bitterness people cling to as they fight in court, hatred and anger catapulting wickedness deeper into already tormented lives. She couldn't imagine them behaving in such a way. Rich was a great guy. She looked at him. What were they doing anyway? The thought occurred to her that he desired a quick divorce to allow the next step to be taken with…whoever she was. She looked away as the feeling of failure crept in for a moment.

Divorcing, that's what they were doing.

They began filling the papers out, one by one. Each document brought deeper discussion and thought into what was necessary to fulfill each person's needs. Kind and courteous yet impersonal, they both worked with a terribly strong sense of disconnect. They were two strangers making major decisions that would affect the lives of each other as well as two children. The feeling was odd, to say the least.

REBECCA L. MATTHEWS

With financial information complete, discussion turned to assets. There would be no alimony. Judy had no interest in tying Rich to her; money was not what was important to her, after all. They both agreed the life insurance, the policies they already had in place, was important to continue as it was. Rich wanted her to keep the house, acknowledging her recent improvements that had made it feel like home to her. She would not attach to his business, and the vehicles would remain as they already were. In order to accomplish separating these assets and to ensure the payments on her car and the house were able to be made, Rich offered a large amount for child support each month—fourteen hundred dollars, as she had already seen. He wanted to be sure their needs were met.

The visitation schedule was easily agreed upon. Rich would have the kids every other weekend, Friday after school until Sunday night at seven thirty. He could take them each Wednesday afternoon for the night, bringing them to school on Thursday mornings if he felt comfortable doing so. Since Rich wanted Judy to continue being home for the kids after school, he offered to do all the traveling to help financially, since her hours at work would remain less than full time. Holidays would alternate; vacations could be decided at any time, taking into consideration each other's plans. All of this schedule would remain flexible.

These discussions were taxing. They never did discuss Rich's affair or Judy's arrogance that led him there.

Time and time again, Judy wanted to ask, but God kept her silent. She excused herself to the restroom only once to regain composure and ask for strength.

Once the paperwork was done, Rich explained they would need to submit it to the court, have their signatures notarized, and await a hearing date to go before a judge to finalize the divorce. Judy so much wanted to get away at this point. Each step seemed to bring them deeper into the unknown. Divorce seemed like something they would not have ever done.

Judy rose from her seat abruptly and stepped to the door. "Can we wait to go to the court tomorrow? I've got to get going now. The kids will be home soon."

"Are you okay?" Reaching for her arm, he touched her sleeve. "Judy, I'm sorry I've hurt you. What we have done here today was good. We can get through all this without a fight."

How ironic. Their life together had been nothing but one big, long fight, and now they were "getting through this" without one.

Taking a deep breath and resuming her composure, Judy answered, "Yes, life does go on."

Judy drove home feeling empty and confused. She trusted in God's ways, but this hurt so much. Rich confused her. Was she missing something? Why was he being so helpful? She was unsure of herself. All she knew and all she had been teetered precariously on the edge of the cliff their marriage was falling off of. How it all would fall, nobody but God really knew.

chapter 18

That night at home, after the children had gone to bed, Judy got out her painting supplies. She laid the foundations of her sadness on canvas. There was no visible picture, no form understood. The colors, their transitions and movement, were symbolic of Judy's struggle between earthly feelings and spiritual belief. Anger and control, sadness and release, and trust and peace all mixed, ebbed, and flowed. The end result was a great visual of life—her life. Stepping back, three hours after beginning, she felt a weight lifted. *What a satisfying feeling*.

This painting became the focal point of her entryway wall. The painting's colors accentuated the color of the floor tiles, offset the walls very nicely, and were an ever-present reminder to Judy to let go and let God.

....

The papers were filed with the court, the visitation schedule was followed, and life continued without disruption.

At work, Judy's coworkers proved a bit bothersome. In an effort to connect more personally with those she cared about, Judy had shared the easy transition of divorcing amicably. Much to her chagrin, they, as a united front, warned her to beware of Rich's intentions.

In their opinions, she should fight for a share of his business. They also believed that alimony was deserved after his infidelity. They felt he couldn't truly be so generous and that he must surely be hiding something. They argued that Judy should hire a lawyer just in case she was being taken advantage of.

Regardless of their attempts, Judy did not pull away from their friendships, nor did she embrace their suggestions. She did defend her husband and continued her spiritual conviction to trust God and let him have control. Firmly, Judy believed, she could stand as an example of what a relationship with God could do. Jamie, however, was becoming quite a concern.

Summer vacation was well underway, and Jamie was filling her quota of negativity, fitting the image of the rebellious teen to a *T*, which she had not been until her parents' separation had become known to her. Nothing her mother could do was right, and though she seemed to accept going on the visits with her father, she had lots to say against the rules at his house.

"Yeah, well, I'm fourteen and should be able to!" Jamie was shouting at her mother again.

"Honey, I'm sorry, but I don't agree." Judy could feel her frustration rising. She was getting tired of these confrontations from her daughter. The separation obviously had been hard on her, and perhaps it was withholding the information to begin with that caused it, but somehow it felt as though Jamie didn't trust her anymore. "I am not comfortable with you hanging out with your friends in town either. It's just not safe."

"It is so safe. What's the big deal? They get to."

"That's another point. You're friends have too much freedom." Judy was bothered a lot by that point. Were parents even involved with this new group of friends Jamie discovered?

"Too much freedom? Give me a break! It's you guys that don't understand it is normal to go out with your friends!" Jamie stormed out of the room, leaving Judy seeking a quiet moment with her Father in prayer.

Judy's painting filled her spare time with meaning and helped to dispel frustrations as they arose. Peter loved to spend hours in his mother's bedroom, sitting on her loveseat drawing while she painted remarkable scenes of landscape.

During summer vacation, while Judy worked, the kids were home alone. Sarah was working full time now, getting ready for her first year of college, so she was not available to watch the kids. Besides, they were getting much too old for that anyway. Judy kept careful tabs on their activities and tried to encourage them to get outside rather than sit in front of the television all day. She worked from nine to two thirty and felt comfortable with the time they were without her. Rich kept them longer on Thursdays, taking them for hikes or shopping. He was being such a help. The summer schedule seemed to work well for all of them.

Peter kept to himself mostly. Though he had friends, he was more of a loner. Jamie, as she became more dismissive of her parents, spent a large amount of time with her friend Stephanie, and she was becoming harder to reach. Judy did ponder on whether these changes would have come anyway. Teenage girls do become rebellious. Perhaps it had little to do with what she and Rich had been going through. The timing could have merely been coincidental.

Stephanie was also found to be rebellious. Judy wasn't sure which of the two girls encouraged the negativity or if they fed off each other's, but when they were together, the atmosphere just felt dark. They didn't care for either Judy's or Rich's rules and seemed to be happy enough pushing the limits. Dirty looks and snappy answers were getting old to all who received them.

When Stephanie stayed over in late July, the two girls snuck out during the night. Judy was awakened at three in the morning only to find the two girls giggling as they came tiptoeing through the front door. Judy was furious. As Jamie's mother, she found herself wanting to believe it was Stephanie's fault and tried to encourage Jamie to find other friends. Grounding her for two weeks did little to improve her attitude.

Rich enforced the same punishment and rules as Judy. They supported each other. This did not help, however, to turn Jamie around. She was mad at her parents for their united "attacks" against her. She was constantly declaring that they were ganging up on her.

As the visitations continued as scheduled, Judy kept waiting to hear word of Rich's girlfriend. Never prying, she was always listening for something to be said by one of the kids. Unless they had kept her a secret, it seemed as though they had yet to be introduced. It was as if the "other woman" didn't even exist. Rich was probably trying to follow a protocol of sorts, making sure one door was firmly and completely closed before opening the next to their children. Judy appreciated his etiquette but was still unsettled about their meeting her in the future. Would Rich continue working together with her in the best interest of the kids, or would the other woman encourage him to parent differently? She could do nothing more than wait to find out.

chapter 19

The court appointed a date for a final hearing of the divorce. It was scheduled for a date early in September, two days after school was to resume. Judy sat in the sanctuary of her bedroom/art studio holding the paper in her hand, unsure of what she was feeling.

Judy's mind wandered back to the night of her spiritual encounter. She thought of the complete change that one moment, one touch of her heart, made in all of their lives. It had been such a sad night; she was at the end of herself, huddled and crying on a dark, deserted road. Brush and trees were holding her in shadow, but light was breaking through. When God made changes to Judy that night, he began at the core of her. He started with a touch that spawned an inner glow. That glow grew and spread throughout her being, which now radiated outward to all.

Standing, placing the court paper aside, Judy gathered her painting supplies. That was the moment that made her who she was today. Brush and palette in hand, she painted.

The trees, the shrubbery, the atmosphere, darkness enveloped all. Evil lurked within each twisted bough, threatening. She painted the broken and crying figure of her old being, naked, huddled on the ground, for that was what she was at that moment in time, exposed and fearful.

That was where she had needed to be, for in that nakedness she had reached out and touched freedom. Being clothed in the image she had created only encouraged the darkness; it strengthened evil's very power. It was in exposure that she was released and freedom tickled life alive from the inside.

Within the naked form Judy created a glow, a visually captivating speck of light. With a touch of the artist's brush, a weak imitation of the holy hand at work, Judy was able to breathe life into her painting. Meaning spread through the strokes of her hand. This depiction of the moment of her transformation would touch many lives. For now, it made her weep.

She, having never done so before, named her painting. It was affectionately and appropriately labeled *The Light Within*. Once it was framed, Judy hung it in her living room, a testament to all of both the end and the beginning of her life.

....

As August slipped away and September chilled the air, school began. Peter began sixth grade and was excited.

Jamie began high school and was scared, though she so much tried to hide it.

The fear Jamie experienced waiting for her first day of school was immense, but it brought with it clarity. She didn't know who she was and, while trying to seek the approval of friends, had alienated herself from those who really loved her. Her parents were finalizing their divorce in two days, and her best friend, Stephanie, didn't seem to care about what that meant for her. She constantly pointed out that her parents were failures too, just like Jamie's.

Jamie did notice something different about her parents, though. They got along very well. They worked together as parents even if it was often to her disadvantage. They both loved her very much and never let their separation change that. Rather, it seemed to help both Peter and her, because due to their parents' breakup, she and Peter had spent the summer getting to know their father.

Jamie now felt guilty for being so mean. This had been her first opportunity to spend real time with her dad, and all she seemed to give him was a hard time.

On the first day of school, Judy drove both Jamie and Peter, dropping Peter off first. Jamie watched her mother give Peter a kiss, a hug, and a wish for a great day. Feeling envious, she watched as he skipped up the steps to the front doors of the grade school in high spirits. Judy turned the car away and drove on to Jamie's school, which was farther away. It was much larger, as it combined three different towns, grades nine through twelve. Jamie was very nervous.

"Mom, do you remember your first day of high school?" Jamie awkwardly asked.

Judy glanced at her daughter, obviously surprised by the question. Jamie had pushed her mother away all summer long. But in her fear she desperately needed to connect with her now. "I guess I remember a bit. I was extremely shy, so I was quite nervous. I remember lining up with my classmates to be introduced as the new freshman class. I remember slipping behind a friend just wanting to hide. But I also ended up loving school, so it must not have been too bad."

"Mom…" Jamie's timid voice drew Judy's eyes once again. "I'm scared."

A tear welled up in Jamie's eye, and her chin trembled as she struggled to contain herself. She felt like a small child. Her tough act was faltering. Judy pulled into the parking lot of the high school, drove to the farthest corner, and stopped the car.

Turning to her trembling child, she reached out and hugged her. Jamie could feel the rebellious tension slip away as the unfamiliar embrace became comforting. Judy shed a tear for her child, shared her fear for the moment, but then sat back to encourage her on her journey. "You will be fine, Jamie."

Her mom's attempts at comforting Jamie seemed to help. She took a deep breath, wiped away her tears, checked her makeup in the mirror, and faced her mother. "How do I look?"

"You look great! You are so beautiful. Be confident; you are an awesome person. High school will be fun for you."

"Thanks, Mom." With another shaky breath, Jamie looked out the window at her new school. "I guess I'm ready to go now."

"Let's not make you late." Judy drove to line up behind the other parents dropping off their children. A boy got out of the car in front of them, and when he turned around, Judy and Jamie looked at each other with surprise.

"Mom, he has a beard." Jamie's voice was tight and squeaky. "I'm too young to be here."

"You'll be fine." As the car before them vacated the drop-off spot, Judy pulled up.

Jamie's heart was racing as she opened the door and got out. She was shaking inside right down to her brand new sneakers. "Bye," she said. Putting on a brave face, she began the walk to the main doors of the high school, following the boy with the beard.

Jamie pulled her frame up taller, and her stride became more confident as she heard her mother slowly drive away.

chapter 20

"Mom, it was awesome!" As she tumbled through the door of their car, these precious words came out of Jamie's mouth.

A warm smile spread across Judy's face as she inwardly acknowledged God's hand in this. Jamie reached over and awkwardly embraced her mother, letting go just as quickly. Tears welled up in Judy's eyes for the touch that she had missed.

The back door opened as Peter crawled in. "I love sixth grade! I have homework already." This was said with a smile, no less.

"You're weird," Jamie exclaimed as she turned to face her brother buckling up in the backseat.

"No, I'm not. I just think it's fun. Mom, can I do my homework in your room?"

"Sure." Judy started the car, leaving the bus stop behind, and headed toward home. "Did you both like your teachers?" This was the second year that Peter had multiple teachers in one day. Jamie had seven classes, and all the teachers were new faces to her.

"I had a new science teacher. Mrs. Tipper moved away over the summer, and they got someone new. I don't remember her name," Peter responded. "I liked most of my teachers. I'm not sure about my English teacher yet; he seems strict."

The school discussion continued with each of them excitedly talking over the other until they reached their house. Snack time was filled with energy. Judy had forgotten how wonderful it was to have both children happy. This was a moment to remember.

"How was Stephanie's day?" Judy inquired of Jamie's best friend.

"I don't know. I didn't see her much. We don't share any classes, but our lockers are near each other. I think I was just too busy trying to figure out what I was supposed to do to talk with her."

Judy felt a bit of excitement—hope, perhaps, that good changes were going to set in for Jamie and her social life. Trying to be bigger than her frustrating irritation at a child, Judy offered good wishes instead. "Well, I hope it was a good day for her as well."

"She knows a bunch of kids at the high school already. I'm sure she had a great day."

This additional information didn't sit well with Judy. It was as if she was seeking red flags in anything when it came to Stephanie. She could do no right in Judy's eyes since the girls had snuck out that summer night. Like Judy had never done anything sneaky as a teenager herself. She certainly had her rebellious moments. Who was she to judge? Perhaps that was why she wanted to shelter her daughter from the consequences of poor choices.

Later, after dinner was over and the kitchen cleaned up, Peter and Judy headed to her bedroom. Jamie had gone to her own bedroom earlier to do her homework. Judy stopped in and offered for her to join her and Peter if she wanted.

"There's lots of room to spread out your homework," Judy suggested.

"I'm all set. Thanks, though." Jamie was sitting on her bed with her history book open on her lap, a notebook beside her, and soft music playing from her radio.

"Suit yourself. I'm gonna go paint." Judy left Jamie to herself and joined Peter, who was already nestled into the comfortable loveseat with a book he was to read for a book report.

Settling in at her easel, Judy sat looking at her blank canvas and wondered what to paint next. She prayed for inspiration. Her door, only slightly ajar, slipped open wider, causing Judy to look up. Her hands full, Jamie pushed the door closed again behind her, joined Peter on the loveseat, and laid her books and papers on the table in front of her.

"I changed my mind." With a timid smile hinting an uncertainty that she was truly welcome, Jamie opened her history book once more.

"I'm so glad you did." Judy beamed, and inspiration was born.

Sketching an outline, Judy felt unsure of her abilities. She had never painted faces before, but then again, she had accomplished beautiful works of art without having had prior experience.

The lines drawn began to take shape, and the contours took on meaning. In the matter of an hour or so, her children's faces graced her canvas. After observing and analyzing her children's expressions and painstakingly replicating their individual features, she was feeling a tad bit emotional, and rightly so. There were so many little details she had familiarized herself with again.

When your baby lies in the crook of your arm, you gaze upon and touch each feature, caress every inch, and fill your heart with knowledge and understanding of who they are. You know your baby completely, as if you are one.

As time insists its presence be acknowledged, your child grows and journeys on. Changes beckon it to become unique, individual, and separate.

Judy still recognized, faint as they were, her babies. The infants within, then nurtured and safe, having since walked through disappointment, achievement, fear, joy and doubt, were still evident to their mother's eye. The artist's eye, however, saw them as the individuals they were becoming. Gracefully, she was portraying them as such, combining image and essence to begin the creation of a beautiful portrait of her children.

"Okay, kids. It's time for dessert and bedtime."

As the kids got their dessert, Judy looked at the calendar hanging in the kitchen. The court hearing was in two days. Butterflies filled her stomach at the reminder. She was glad for what their separation had done, for all of them, glad for the relationships they had all created. She was sad for what was ending. Marriage should be forever, but it should be filled with love, unconditional love. The difficult marriage they had shared was coming to a close, but also being shut was the window of hope Judy held for reconciliation.

chapter 21

Judy was standing nervously, feeling as if she were watching herself in a dream. The judge beckoned them to sit. Judy looked meekly at Rich, who sat at a large table separate from hers. This was symbolic of their life at this moment. Though they had worked together to create the documents, though they had parented together through this difficult summer, they now stood opposing each other in a court of law. The opposition wasn't heated, of course, but they were no longer united.

The judge glanced through the papers before him. He was speaking, something about irreconcilable differences. Judy was having difficulty focusing her attention. Reality was blurry. The judge looked up, over the document in his hand, to take in the sight of the two before him. Judy felt guilty in this setting.

"Do you both agree that this marriage is beyond repair?" His voice was intimidating.

Rich answered quickly, "I do."

Ironic words, Judy thought. She was a bit more hesitant. "I agree." The two words escaped her lips as they began to tremble.

Rich smiled at her, but his face held a wince of pain. Judy looked quizzically back. She was sorry for how she had treated him. She had said it time and time again. He should be happy he was now being set free to live the life he had begun over four years earlier.

The judge reiterated the basic information outlining assets, child support, and visitation schedules. Rich and Judy acknowledged their agreement to the terms they had previously decided together.

In closing, the judge addressed them directly. "Many couples have crossed these floors, lawyers and agendas in tow. They fight and seek to hurt as much as they can. In the process, many of them victimize their children, creating scars that will never heal. Very seldom do I face a couple such as yourselves who choose to put their differences aside and work together for the good of their children. It is too bad you couldn't have communicated better during your marriage and avoided this end result. I grant this divorce based on irreconcilable differences as you have requested. You will receive your final documents in the mail."

With a drop of the gavel, their lives were now separate. The judge rose and left the room through a door located behind his desk.

Judy sat once more, trembling deep inside. Rich rose and came to stand at her table, offering a feeble smile. "See, that wasn't so bad."

Judy looked up at him, wanting to shake her head in disbelief. The judge had been right. If their communication had been good, Rich would never have sought another woman, they would be together and happy, and their family would be intact. Rich seemed callous to what had just taken place, but perhaps his needs were now being met. Judy stood. Her feelings were hurt.

Suppressing the urge to make a smart remark, she smiled weakly instead and spoke in truth, "It's been good for the kids." Feeling the need to escape, she continued, "Speaking of which, I've got to get home. I'll see you later." Turning, Judy walked with her head held high through the grand corridors of the courthouse, out the arched doorway and home to her new life, determined to remain supportive of Rich unconditionally.

When the bus arrived, Judy was waiting. Peter and Jamie knew what was happening today for their parents. They were quiet when they got in the car.

Jamie inquired, "How did it go?"

"Everything went fine. Nothing has changed, of course; the decisions we made together are what we will be following. Your visits and stuff, I mean. The divorce is final." Judy had said the words they were all dreading to hear.

"Mom, are you all right?" Peter was so sweet; he always seemed to care about others first.

"Yes, I'm fine. As I said, nothing has changed for us. Are you guys ready to go?"

"Buckled, I'm ready," voiced Peter from the backseat.

"Buckled, I'm ready," chimed Jamie from beside Judy, reliving a ritual they used to follow when they were much younger. This brought a smile to Judy's face. She remained quiet, though, lost in thought. It was final, and it felt significant. As this fact settled in, there was a touch of boldness, an air of excitement. What was behind her was past; she was to live in the here and now, embrace each day for what God brought her. She felt as though the future was laid out before her; she could do anything and be anything. She felt bold and strong. The kids watched her as she sat a bit taller and allowed the hint of an inward smile to tug at the corners of her mouth.

chapter 22

Life did go on. Judy enjoyed work and spending time with her coworkers each day, came home to her wonderful children each afternoon, and enjoyed the time God provided for her to be alone. She had spent time working on the painting of her children, difficult as she found it to be. She so much wanted to portray them as accurately as she could, reflecting who they were, inside and out. It would prove to be an ongoing project, often put aside to work on other paintings as images compelled her to illustrate them.

Weeks turned into months as Jamie's fifteenth birthday passed and the holidays came and went. Judy was thrilled at the growth of the relationships between her children and their father. She was aware, however, that another woman had still not been brought into their lives. None that was mentioned at least, not that she asked.

Within all the good, there was one concern nagging at Judy: Jamie's growing social struggle. School didn't seem to present a problem. Her grades were good, and she liked her teachers. She seemed torn when it came to her friend Stephanie. Stephanie's rebellious behavior and the freedom allowed her by her parents often conflicted with Jamie's personality. Jamie was trying to be a good kid and make wise choices but was easily tempted, or taunted, into joining Stephanie and her older friends' misguided behaviors.

....

Hanging in the halls at school between classes one day, Jamie found herself caught up in the gang's attempt to bully Sam, a fellow freshman. He was timid and looked scared. Jamie, not daring to stand up for him yet not able to walk away, found herself in the crowd opposing him. They knocked the books out of his hands, and papers became strewn on the floor. In a desperate attempt to avoid looking at them, Sam scrambled about grasping at papers. Jim, the oldest and meanest of the group, took advantage of Sam's position and, using his black-soled boot, shoved him flat to the ground, holding him down. Everyone laughed except Jamie. She was horrified.

A teacher walking down the crowded hall caught sight of the loud group and, interested to see what they were circled around, headed in their direction. After a loud warning from someone in the crowd, they all dispersed quickly, leaving Sam to pick himself and his papers up in tears. Jamie, seeing the full effect of the actions she'd participated in and knowing the penalty for her role, chose not to flee. She knelt at Sam's side and, with tears in her own eyes, gathered up papers for him.

Mrs. Hayes reached the pair and asked what had happened. Jamie explained, as best as she could, while fully implicating herself. Sam, sniffling, was too afraid to point a finger at any of them. He knew his days would be numbered if he did.

Jamie was sent to the office to meet with the guidance counselor. This school stood by a zero tolerance standard for bullying. However, regardless of the years the students were told this, the bullies still seemed to rule. Jamie's mother arrived within twenty minutes to claim her daughter, who was being suspended for the remainder of the week.

After having spent fifteen minutes listening to the guidance counselor reiterate the school's policy on bullying followed by a brief report that Jamie and her friends had ganged up on a fellow student, they began a tense ride home. "What is going on, Jamie?"

"I don't know," Jamie answered softly.

"What do you mean, you don't know?" Judy's confusion was turning to anger, and she could do little to hide it.

"All right, you don't have to flip out about it!" Jamie's smart remark now found her treading on dangerous ground.

Judy focused her eyes on the road ahead and took some slow, deep breaths. She remained in quiet contemplation the remainder of the ride and throughout the rest of the day at home.

That night, at bedtime, Judy went to Jamie's room and sat beside her on her bed. Jamie chose not to acknowledge her mother's presence.

After a few minutes, Judy broke the silence. "I'm sorry if you feel I don't understand you."

"Mom, you weren't even going to listen; I could tell right away!"

"I'm confused. I know you and Stephanie are still friends, but bullying just isn't who you are. I can't even picture you doing that."

"I didn't know what to do. They're wicked mean." Jamie looked down at her hands, wringing them nervously. "It doesn't matter. They're gonna get me now, anyway."

"What do you mean they're going to get you?" Judy sounded concerned but also confused.

"I told on them. I felt so bad for Sam. He was crying, and they didn't even care. It was almost as if they liked it."

"You told on them? The guidance counselor didn't tell me that."

"I was helping Sam pick up his papers when Mrs. Hayes asked him what happened. He wouldn't tell her, so I did. She sent me to Mr. Gooden. Since I was part of the crowd, they were my friends, and I didn't step in to stop them, I got in trouble."

"Jamie, I'm proud of you for telling the truth. That is important, even if you get in trouble." Turning to face her daughter, Judy continued with a smile of encouragement. "I'm sorry I wasn't in a place to listen earlier." Judy patted Jamie's leg affectionately. "I can't imagine how you must have felt. You must have been scared."

Jamie shrugged. "No big deal." Truthfully, she was scared to death, but she couldn't share that with her mother. As a bystander, she was in trouble but got off easy for staying behind to help. Her reduced sentence also was going to be seen as a bold statement that she had ratted out her "friends." The looks they gave her as they filtered into the office to face their own penalties were far from friendly.

She realized that the day had come to take a stand for what was right. She wished so much that she could relive last summer. If only she had stayed close to her mom. If only she had kept away from Stephanie back then. She had only wanted to fit in, and acting rebellious seemed to be what was cool, in Stephanie's eyes, anyway.

chapter 23

"Hi, Rich, how are you?" Judy's voice sounded troubled.

"I'm good. Is everything okay?"

"That's why I'm calling. I was called to the school today. Jamie got suspended."

Rich felt a jolt of shock. His daughter was a good kid. "What do you mean? What happened?"

Judy explained the bullying incident as Jamie had told it to her. Rich felt better as he realized his daughter was making good choices, even though she got in trouble. "How is she doing?"

"She seems upset, but she says she's fine. I'm so angry at that Stephanie."

"I guess I feel the same. I wish she'd never gotten mixed up with that group." Truthfully, Rich harbored anger toward himself about the whole situation. If he had remained faithful, their home life would have been much healthier, and their daughter wouldn't have clung to such a mean girl. He felt quite sure of that. "I was so glad when it seemed as though they weren't close anymore. Boy, was she tough to handle over the summer. They both were."

"No kidding. I couldn't get over how difficult Jamie got. She fought with me about everything it seemed."

They talked for over an hour about their children and hung up. Rich felt stronger and encouraged about Jamie's future choices. She really was, after all, a great girl.

Rich and Judy had kept in touch regularly. Their discussions encompassed their kids' grades, behaviors, schedules, appointments, and health. They laughed over them, released frustration over them, and even disagreed at times about them. They were both so closely knit in the parenting of their children that, in the eyes of Jamie and Peter, they were one family.

They'd talked more in the last six months than they had in years as a married couple. The focus, however, never left the children. To offer his respect for Judy and her space, Rich had never approached the door of the house he used to live in. He always called to be sure the kids were ready for him, and they always came out when he arrived to pick them up.

Judy deserved so much better than he had given her. He wanted to allow her all the personal space and privacy she might need to start a new life with someone else. That was why he kept the conversations to the children. He wondered why he had never heard of anyone new in their children's lives, in Judy's life. He so much wanted her to be happy.

Judy was a wonderful person; she was always uplifting and positive. Rich struggled inside with a deep sadness for what he had done and the separation it had caused. It was like his life had been torn in two. It hurt to hide behind the veil of smiles when the kids were over, and it was more difficult to listen to her voice as they talked so often and not reach out for her. He could not allow himself to cross the boundary that he had laid so carefully. If he did, he felt it would risk infringing on her freedom to find new love, a love she so deeply deserved. He had to keep their relationship focused on the children only, for her sake.

....

Peter's twelfth birthday was coming up on February 20. Judy had some ideas for gifts but wanted his opinion on party options.

"How about having a slumber party? You could invite a few friends and sleep on the living room floor watching movies all night."

"I don't know." Peter didn't seem all that interested in her suggestion. Judy had known that his birthday had been on his mind a lot; he mentioned it at least twice daily.

Frowning a bit in confusion, Judy tried another route. "How about a pool party?" Surely that was an exciting idea.

"I don't think so."

"I'm confused. Do you want a party at all?" Judy couldn't imagine this opportunity passing him by. He had different friends over throughout the school year and seemed to enjoy himself with them. They rarely went swimming at The Swimming Hole, the athletic club downtown, so that would certainly be a treat.

"I do. I want a party," Peter said excitedly with a grin.

He had his mother's attention now. "Then what is it you have in mind?"

"I want a party with just my family, here at home."

Judy was confused. "Okay. That is not so exciting or extraordinary. Are you sure?"

"Yup, I want a family party here, but I want Dad to come. That would be all of my family, making it a *real* family party."

"Oh, I see. I'm not quite sure that's such a good idea," Judy said quietly as thoughts filled her mind.

That was the bombshell. Judy had believed the boundary laid by her ex-husband was purposeful. She had never questioned him about it, just respected it. Her belief was that he was keeping his lady friend private, enjoying their time together when he didn't have the kids. Rich joining them at this house for Peter's party would be good for Peter but perhaps not so good for the adults. She didn't want to make waves and felt uncomfortable suggesting this to Rich.

"Why not? It's what I want for my birthday." Peter frowned.

"We are divorced, you understand. Daddy has his life, and I have mine. I don't join you at his home, and he doesn't visit us here. That's what happens when parents divorce." Judy touched Peter's sleeve.

"You don't fight at all. You talk all the time." Peter was defensive and willing to argue his point.

"We don't fight, and that's good. We talk about you two." She turned him to face her.

"Right, this is about one of us two." Sadness as well as anger laced his words.

"How long have you been thinking about this?" Judy was curious as she watched Peter's face. The smile and excitement were now gone, replaced with a look of loss.

"For a while, I guess. I want to be with all of you, at one time. I don't want to have a party here and then a party there. Let's just all be together and do it once."

"Most kids would love two parties. Just imagine that you could get two times the stuff!" Judy was feeling discouraged. She felt the sound of bribery slip past her lips and hated it.

Peter folded his arms and hung his head in defeat. "I'm not most kids."

Well, he is right there. He most certainly wasn't like most kids. He wasn't very social, he wasn't fond of sports, he liked to read more than play video games, and he loved being with his family. Judy couldn't hold back a smile as she pondered on who her son was. She liked who he was.

"Okay, I'll talk with your father. Let me see how he feels about it." Judy couldn't help giving in. It obviously meant so much to Peter.

"Hooray!" He jumped up, and after a kiss and big hug, he skipped out of the room, leaving his mother behind.

How was she supposed to talk about this with Rich? Just the thought brought butterflies to her stomach.

chapter 24

Jamie had returned to school the following week, her punishment obligation met. She was afraid of running into the gang. Quickly though, she realized that Jim, Stephanie, and most of the gang were still out on suspension, so she had at least a couple of days to be who she wanted to be without fear. She stepped forward, bold and strong, embraced each class, and listened with a new fervor to each teacher.

She had a new goal in life, and it wasn't to appease anyone else, especially the bad crowd. She had clung deep to the realization that she could be whoever she wanted. Peer pressure didn't need to apply; she was going to follow her heart.

As the day's classes came to a close and Jamie climbed aboard her bus, she felt a strong sense of satisfaction. She had organized her locker, cleaned out the clutter, and brought home homework that wasn't even due yet, confident her grades would reflect her new excitement. Her grades weren't terribly bad to begin with, but she knew she had much more to offer.

Her mother was, as always, at the bus stop waiting for Peter and her to arrive. She smiled as the bus came to a stop. She used to hate that her mother was there every day. She felt trapped, like she had no freedom. It was almost embarrassing. Now she kind of liked it.

Even though it had been wrong for Sam to be bullied, the whole episode helped her to see the direction she had been heading in. The last week spent deep in soul-searching thought and prayer made her appreciate the simple life she had. Her mother loved her, sappy as it was, and she was glad that she cared enough to be at this bus stop every day.

Jamie slid into the seat beside her mother with a smile on her face.

"How did it go? Your first day back, I mean," Judy asked.

Jamie chose to keep her newfound direction close to her heart for now. "It was fine."

"Hello, Mom!" Peter climbed in the backseat, gaining the ladies' attention with his cheerfulness.

Judy smiled as she watched him. "Hi, Peter. How was school for you?"

"Great! We had a fire drill today. That was fun!"

Returning her attention back to Jamie while Peter buckled up, Judy continued with their conversation. "Fine? What about Stephanie? Did you have any trouble with her or her friends?"

"They're still out on suspension," Jamie reminded her mother.

"Oh, that's right. You had a 'lighter sentence,' as you put it, didn't you? Be sure you let me, or a teacher, know if they are any trouble to you when they come back."

"Sure, Mom." Jamie closed her mother off subtly, ending the conversation by placing her iPod ear buds in her ears.

"So you had a fire drill today? How exciting for you."

"Yeah, it was a mistake, though. The lunch ladies burned something. The fire trucks came and everything. It was so cool! We were cold outside because we'd been in music class when it happened. We didn't have our coats. That's why it was so fun. Everyone was chattering, like this." Judy looked back briefly to see his bared teeth as Peter made an effort to chatter like he was freezing.

Jamie listened as her brother and mother talked while her music softly played. They brought a smile to her lips. She loved her family.

....

As had become their ritual, they all settled into Judy's studio after dinner. Peter had his sketchpad out, attempting some creativity with pastels this time. Jamie had her homework spread out and was diligently working. Judy sat behind her easel facing the two of them. The warm feeling this atmosphere lent led her to set their unfinished portrait back before her.

She had come a long way but had usually finished a painting in a few sittings at the most; none had ever taken this long. This one intimidated her. What she had been missing was this—this feeling of contentment, that everything was right in their world. She got her paints out and gazed upon the pair endearingly. She captured these feelings, this moment of timelessness, and her deep love and affection, within the expressions of her two children's faces. In less than an hour she had accomplished her goal; the portrait was now finished.

In the painting, Jamie's expression was subdued and thoughtful, her features strong yet beautiful, fully representing the person she truly was. Peter's face was enlightened and cheerful. A small touch of a smile hinted at the corners of his mouth, but his eyes were squinted and arched in absolute joy, a reflection of his inner child.

Judy was so pleased with this painting. Looking into the likeness of the faces of her children, she could feel them. She looked past the canvas, seeing them comfortable in her space. Life felt so full at that moment. God was so good.

She held the painting up, clearing her throat for attention. Each child had been deep in concentration, focused intently on their projects. Clearing her throat once again, Judy called for attention. "Excuse me, children. I would like your attention, please."

They looked up, and their mouths opened in awe at their images before them.

"Oh my goodness!" Jamie exclaimed.

"Wow! Mom, that's good!" Peter jumped up from the couch, spilling his pastels in the process. "Can I see that next to me in the mirror?"

Carefully carrying the painting, hoping not to drop it or smudge it, Judy held it beside her son's face so he could compare. Even she was amazed. She had never painted before these past six months. Pencil sketches as a child, often left incomplete, had been the extent of her artistic adventures. God really did bless what she had chosen to do, just as he said he would.

Jamie came to stand on the other side in the mirror, beside her image. "That's really cool, Mom. How did you ever learn to do that kind of stuff?"

"It is purely a gift from God, Jamie, a gift from God."

chapter 25

It was the call she had dreaded making. Judy had to discuss Peter's upcoming birthday party with Rich.

Rich answered after only two rings. "Hey there."

Judy hesitated briefly, hearing the excitement in her ex-husband's voice. "Hi, Rich."

"Hey, Judy, I thought you were one of the kids calling. What's up?"

He sounded so casual. When they were married she had loved the deep, smooth, soothing tone of his voice—when they weren't arguing, that is. How should she begin? "I want to talk about Peter's birthday."

"Okay. About presents, I'm not quite sure what I'm gettin' him yet."

"Oh," Judy responded.

"Do you know what you're getting him? We don't want to get him the same thing, huh? That would be funny, wouldn't it?"

Judy answered Rich's question first. "I guess I was thinking of getting him an art set: an easel, water paints, brushes, pad of paper. He is very artistic." Judy could imagine the two of them set up to paint together in the studio with a still life model, perhaps the basic fruit in a bowl, arranged on the table between them. She smiled at the camaraderie this vision evoked.

"Oh, yeah, I guess I have noticed that he draws a lot. He does it on our napkins whenever we eat out." Rich chuckled. His laughter sounded so pleasant.

Judy explained some background for him. "I took up painting when you started having the kids over at your place. A little hobby to fill in the quiet time. Peter seems to have taken to it as well."

"That's neat." Rich paused as if in thought. "I guess I didn't know that you painted. Well, I'm not quite sure what I should get him. He likes to read. Maybe I'll get him an assortment of books and magazines. It doesn't sound like a lot of fun, though, does it?"

"I think he'd be thrilled." Judy thought of all the times Peter sat on her loveseat reading. He really did enjoy it. Though happily sidetracked, Judy took a breath and attempted to redirect her focus. "Anyway, that wasn't really what I needed to talk to you about. It's about what he wants to do for his party."

"He wants something extravagant, doesn't he? I can help cover the costs. Let me guess, a movie party like some of his friends have done at the theater."

"No, that's not it. And I'm all set with money. Thanks, though. I did offer to take him and his friends to The Swimming Hole too, but that's not what he wants either."

"Does he want to play indoor mini golf? What else would he want to do? Hmm, I know. How about a tour at the museum? I don't know about his friends, but I bet he would like that." Rich wasn't letting Judy get a word in edgewise.

"I'm sure he would. Rich…" Judy's stomach was in knots at this point. "Peter wants a family party."

"Oh?" Rich sounded confused.

"Here, with you." Judy waited for his reaction.

"Oh." Rich's confusion turned to surprise. "What did you say to that?"

Judy paused then filled the lingering silence. "I told him that we have separate lives and that is what happens when parents divorce."

"What did he think of that?"

"That this is what he wants for his birthday, his family, all of us. He was so cute and so confident. I know this probably would feel awkward for you, but you are welcome to come." Judy held her breath.

"Judy, are you sure you would be comfortable? The last time I was there, well, that was a long time ago."

"I guess I'm okay with it if you are." She felt the movement. The invisible yet tangible lines placed ever so delicately to divide them were shifting.

"If you're sure you wouldn't mind, then let him know I'd be happy to be there."

Judy could hear the smile in his voice and thought to add, "By the way, a gift certificate for the museum sounds like a great idea."

"Not to change the subject, but how is school going for Jamie so far this week? She did just return yesterday, didn't she?" Rich asked.

"She seems a bit distant, happy but distant. The other kids, I think, will be back to school tomorrow or Thursday. I'm not really sure. I know they got longer suspensions than Jamie. She mentioned last week when she got in trouble that 'they were going to get her.'"

"What is that supposed to mean?"

"She didn't offer much more than that, but it sounded to me as though, since she gave their names and they got in trouble, she expects she will be targeted by this group of kids. I told her to let me know and to let a teacher know right away if they bother her."

"I would imagine the school officials would keep their eye on this. I'm sure she'll be fine."

Rich sounded reassuring, but Judy knew Stephanie was a rough kid. "You're probably right. I'll let Peter know that you'll plan to be here on his birthday. I guess we could shoot for five o'clock. We'll have dinner, presents, and then cake. Sound okay?"

"Sounds great. Not terribly exciting for a kid, but if that's his birthday wish, then it shall be granted. Bye." Rich hung up, leaving Judy a touch excited yet nervous, now in a new way.

What would he think coming back in the house? Had it changed much? She wandered around, looking at the house as if she were a stranger again. She had done a good enough job keeping up the housekeeping. Less stuff truly was better. Things had changed a bit, reflecting the calmer and more peaceful side of who she was now, grounded in Christ.

chapter 26

Jamie was beside herself with fear. Knots tightened her stomach. Nausea crouched, ever present, beckoning her to remain alert. She had not known really what to expect when they came back, but their presence at every turn warned her she was in trouble.

She stood at her locker, exchanging books for her next class, and could sense the evil lurking. The air was thick, heightening all of her senses. In all, eight other kids got in trouble for bullying Sam. The web of loyalty had spread further, though. She was not well liked now.

Glancing down to the far end of the hall, she caught a glimpse of Sam at his locker. He looked as timid as she now felt. His hunched shoulders gave her strength, though, reminding her of why she stood against them.

Bang!

Jamie jumped, startled by the sudden sound of her locker door being slammed shut. Jim, the head honcho, and two of his cronies, Derek and Tim, were laughing and jabbing at each other as they continued past her. As she watched them walking away, Jim turned, giving her a glare that hinted of warning.

Jamie locked eyes with Sam, who had turned to see what the commotion was. Quickly, he looked away, closed his locker, and shuffled to his next class, avoiding her scared look.

"Hey, girls, can I sit with you?" Stephanie drew attention to herself at lunch when she joined a group sitting just beyond where Jamie had settled. These girls, not necessarily popular or noticed, sounded quite excited to have her join them. Stephanie's attention was sought out by many, mostly because kids were afraid to be on her bad side. Nobody wanted to be targeted by the bullies, and, sad as it was, it was better to be acquaintances than enemies.

"Oh my God, look at your necklace. I love it!" Quite a bit louder than she needed to be, Stephanie was fawning over them. They giggled in return. Often she would look up to be sure Jamie was paying attention.

She was. She was now the outcast.

Over the next week or so, the jabs were more directly felt by Jamie. The looks came from many directions, the whispering ceased in many a hushed conversation when she walked into a classroom, and she was bumped into more times than she could count.

Jamie felt alone standing against this great giant. The school days were filled with threats seemingly seen by nobody but her. The controller in Stephanie had refused to share Jamie with anyone else while they were friends. Now that they were enemies, Jamie had no one else. That was the crux of partnering with evil.

Jamie was hurting. By day she was overwrought with stress; by night, she was sleepless and scared.

It was a night such as this, ten days into the worst experience of her life, that she lay in bed crying. She gave in to the fear, gave up on standing strong, and was sick of feeling queasy with torment. She sobbed deeply and angrily.

....

Judy was stirred awake at one o'clock in the morning by a knock at her bedroom door. It had sounded real. It was real enough to drag her up out of a deep, dream-filled sleep, but when she reached the door, no one was there. Standing in confusion, she decided to check on the kids.

Peter was sleeping soundly and looked so peaceful, but light was coming from around the cracks of Jamie's closed door. Judy turned the knob and peered around the edge of the door. In case she was sleeping, Judy whispered, "Jamie, are you okay?"

Jamie rolled away from her mother and pulled her covers up tight to her chin.

"Honey, are you crying?"

Jamie still didn't answer. Judy wondered how long she had been awake. Sitting down on the edge of her bed, she leaned forward to get a better look at her daughter's tear-stained face.

"What's wrong?" Judy was concerned. Jamie had been quiet about school, seemed to focus on homework when she was home, and Rich hadn't mentioned noticing anything wrong when they spent the weekend at his house. Here it was Thursday night, just over two weeks since the incident at school, and Judy had a strong sense this was the issue that had her daughter crying. Pulling her shoulder to encourage her to face her and open up, Judy smiled gently.

"Mom, I don't know what to do. I'm scared. They're so mean." Jamie sniffled and shuddered with a loud sob.

"Mean to you or mean in general?" Judy was concerned.

"To me. Of course they are mean in general. Always mean in general." Jamie's shuddered intakes of breath indicated that she had been sobbing deeply for some time, hyperventilated and broken.

"I'll be right back. We need to talk." Judy left, fighting the fury rising within, to get a cup of water for her daughter and for some one-on-one with God for herself. *Father, give me wisdom and strength. Through you, let me help my child. I'm furious for her pain, and because of that, I need help to step back. This is her walk, not mine.* Bowing at the sink, cup of water now in hand, she finished, *Thank you, Father.*

chapter 27

Jamie chuckled to herself. She was free. Fear was dispelled, and she stood strong on the side of all that was good and right. The gang all seemed to be getting angrier, but they were not getting to her anymore. In fact, it was quite the opposite. She felt a compassion for them she could not have ever felt before. The more she cared, the more irate they became.

They were a sorry group, the lot of them. She felt the most for Stephanie, of course. They had been close, and she had gotten to know a lot about her during their friendship. She understood a lot more of why she acted the way she did, having inside information.

Her mother was right. "Put a face on the enemy," she had said. Jamie knew that her mother focused a lot on God and that kind of stuff, but she had never told her what she should believe in. In a sense, her mother's life was now the example she needed to move forward.

Judy had sat up with Jamie the rest of that Thursday night and had allowed her to stay home on Friday to make up for the lack of sleep. The two of them had lots to talk about.

A lot of what her mother had said made sense. In the days the gang was taunting her, Jamie had figured out a lot, but the pieces fit together much more closely once her eyes were opened spiritually.

For everyone, timing was everything. This was Jamie's time, and as is often the case, tragedy brought clarity.

Judy explained her belief that psychologically, bullies don't bully out of confidence. It is their own insecurity that compels them. Most likely, as Judy pointed out, they were or still are mistreated and made to feel worthless by someone else, often within their own homes.

Jamie was saddened to think of that scenario.

Stephanie had it tough at her house, Jamie was sure of that. She never went there because Stephanie said she was embarrassed by her "stupid parents." Maybe there was more to the story. Maybe she was being mistreated. Her tough demeanor may have been her attempt to stand taller than reality truly felt to her.

Spiritually, Judy went on to explain, you can look at your enemy differently by putting a face on them. Satan is your enemy. He will do anything in his power to deny you the joy that Christ offers, even using people to hurt you, sometimes even the people you care about and are close to. Once you recognize who the enemy really is, you can have compassion on the victims he works through. They are likely not aware of his control. They cannot even fathom what joys they could experience if the enemy within them were exposed and dismissed.

Judy reminded Jamie of the misery they lived in when she "danced with the devil" herself. She had been very controlling, demanding, and even demeaning to all of them. She had been a bully in their home. She reminded Jamie that both she and Peter had acted out a lot in response to her treatment of them and the fighting she used to engage in with their father.

Judy shared the spiritual meanings behind two of her paintings, the personal touch of God that gave her his peace and the light that seemed intertwined with darkness in her life until she was freed and trusted God with her life.

Jamie began to see her own life very differently. She thought on the incident at school, the bullying by her friends, and the bad childhood she had endured. She put these into perspective. Balanced delicately with the changes in her mother, the newfound closeness to her father, and the tugging at her own heart, Jamie's understanding of God and the power of a trusting relationship with him began to take root.

Judy shared with Jamie the story from her Bible of Jesus's sacrifice for all. She pointed out that God's forgiveness of sin, ours and even those who hurt us, should always be revered. She shared personal stories as they related to her walk with Christ. Jamie asked many questions, hungry to learn. Knowing how powerful, personal, and real God truly is, Judy directed her daughter to seek him for her answers. It was necessary that she experience the power of his wisdom for herself. She left her Bible with her and gave her time alone.

Since that long weekend at home with her mother, Jamie had returned to school rejuvenated. She became close to her teachers who, now being aware of the negativity peppered throughout their classrooms and hallways, became more present to and supportive of the seemingly weaker population of students.

She began spending time with the principal and the guidance counselor, working on forming a group for students so that they might feel more confident and secure in their school. This group would hopefully be made up of a mixture of students and faculty set on reducing the reign of intimidation in their halls. Since Jamie had been well marked and was known by all for being a "rat," she stood well as the spokesperson, encouraging others to join her.

The platform that evil had put her on, intending for her to suffer, lifted her high enough to be looked up to by many others who were also plagued by insecurity and fear caused by the bullies in their midst.

The first meeting of this new support group was to be held on February 18. Jamie was excited. As her confidence grew, the anger of Jim, Stephanie, Derek, Tim, and all their friends was amplified. Satan hated a confrontation, or perhaps he liked it. Jamie wasn't quite sure which it was. Confidently, she marched on with God by her side.

Truth be told, she carried a secret hope in her heart. If insecurity plagued the bullies, then really this group was for them. She wished they could stand up against their own foes, in confidence, and let them have control no more. How many children were suffering at home only to take it out on others at school? What a vicious cycle. She wanted it broken.

chapter 28

"I call to order the first meeting of The Steadfast United."

Jamie was dreaming. She was standing before an audience of excited kids in the school auditorium while teachers stood looking on with smiles on their faces. They were not standing guard, searching the crowd for trouble; they were part of the group committing together to stand up against bullying, once and for all.

Just as everyone began to cheer, the fire alarm went off. As the throng of people filtered out to leave the building, Jamie saw Stephanie standing next to the emergency alarm she had just pulled. She was grinning at Jamie, making sure Jamie knew who really was in control.

The alarm heard in the dream was really Jamie's alarm clock beckoning her awake, pulling her out of the disappointment she felt as she looked at her friend's face. She was up now, a bit nervous. Today was the day, February 18.

Peter came barreling through her bedroom door. "Two days left and I can't wait!"

Jamie smiled and ruffled his head. Her brother was growing up quickly. *Twelve.* She remembered when they were younger. They used to fight a lot back then. It really hadn't been long ago. Now she felt so much love toward him. He was special, such a great kid. He was always positive. "Yup, two more days," she said as she released a foot from her covers to step out of bed.

....

This proved to be a tough day to get through; classes seemed to drag on so slowly. She was nervous but excited. Her mother had wished her luck and given her a hug before school and said she would pick her up at four when the meeting was expected to be over.

There was now only one more hour until the final bell of the day. Jamie was finding it hard to concentrate. As the school day ended and the buses filled up, Jamie caught sight of Stephanie in the hall. She looked so sad and empty. Seeing her sadness compelled Jamie to go to her.

"Are you all right?"

Stephanie looked up in surprise and then furrowed her brows in irritation. "What do you want?"

"You look like something's wrong. You know, no matter what you feel about me, I still care about you."

"Huh. You're a little rat. Do you know how much trouble I got in because of you?"

Jamie hadn't thought of that aspect before. If the home lives of these kids were really questionable, most of them probably got in a lot of trouble, the kind many of us would never experience. "Stephanie, it wasn't because of me. It was because of a choice we all made. Own your own mistakes, okay?" With that said, Jamie turned to head to the library, where her meeting was to begin in fifteen minutes.

Stephanie reached out and held Jamie's sleeve, not wanting her to leave. "Wait. I miss you." Stephanie's voice was quiet and cautious but seemed sincere.

"What's wrong, Stephanie? Why aren't you with your friends? Where are Jim and the others?" Jamie looked around as if they might just be lurking close by.

"I don't know. I don't much care either." She didn't sound angry, more like she was struggling with her feelings. "Listen, Jim has told me we're forming a group with allegiances and everything. We're gonna make a pact. It would be more or less the enemy to whatever you're doing. I have a bad feeling about this."

"So don't join." The answer seemed simple enough, but Jamie remembered well the hold darkness had on her not long before.

"Huh. They would never let me go peacefully, you know." There was a hint of fear in Stephanie's eyes as she glanced up to look at Jamie.

"Steph, come with me. My meeting is starting in a few minutes. Don't let them take away your freedom to make your own choices." Jamie was feeling more confident than ever in her mission. She felt bad for Stephanie but could do nothing more than encourage her. Her choices still remained her own to make.

"I gotta go," Stephanie said with a defeated tone. She quickly walked away.

She watched her until she turned the corner at the end of the hall and disappeared. Jamie went to the library and sat down at the head of a long table. She muttered a prayer under her breath for strength and direction for this meeting and for Stephanie.

A quiet voice caught Jamie's attention. "Hi, Jamie."

She looked up to find Sam coming through the library door, the first kid to join her. "Hi, Sam. How are you?"

"Fine. I wanted to thank you for helping me that day. I feel bad for all you've had to put up with since then with those guys."

She shrugged her shoulders. "All for a reason. Are you here for the meeting?" She had made flyers and plastered the walls with them; the invitation should have been clear to all.

He shrugged, his hands buried deep in his pockets. "Yeah, I thought I'd join you since you stuck your neck out for me."

Jamie smiled at his timidity. "Thanks. Anybody else coming that you know?"

"I don't talk to too many kids. I kind of keep to myself, ya know."

Sam was always alone when Jamie saw him. "That's okay," she said. She indicated the chairs, offering for him to join her. The door opened then, and a few more kids filtered in, taking seats at the long table. Mr. Gooden, the guidance counselor, and Mrs. Hayes entered as well. In a matter of five more minutes, the room was buzzing with mild chatter from a group of ten kids and three adults. Jamie rose to greet the crowd with a shaky voice.

"Hi, everyone, I'm Jamie Parker. Thank you for coming." Jamie could feel the heat flush her cheeks and she took a deep breath before continuing. "My goal in starting this group is to educate people about tolerance. I want this group to set an example by getting to know and support one another regardless of similarities or differences. I feel that being generally accepted as an individual would encourage someone to be strong enough to ignore or even avoid peer pressure. I want these meetings open for people to discuss bullying experiences, social as well as personal." Jamie looked around at her captive audience and felt a surge of confidence as she continued, "As a group, we should offer positive encouragement and advice for all who deal with these situations." Jamie noticed a girl's hand up that she did not recognize and called on her.

"You mention tolerance and avoiding peer pressure, but the bullying problem in our school is big.

How can we simply avoid it? Should we? Maybe we need to give them back what they deserve."

Jamie felt a bit uncomfortable but had planned boundaries for these meetings. "I am concerned about them too, obviously, but the reason I am having this meeting is to find positive solutions, not negative." Jamie went on to share her newfound conviction that bullies are people who are also hurting inside. "They are probably bullied themselves, possibly since they were very young and maybe in their very own homes. Judgment and hatred toward them should be replaced by compassion." Jamie heard some mumbling from her audience, so she waited for their attention again before continuing. "Firm boundaries, though, need to be made and well understood. The fear we experience as victims can be redirected as our perceptions of bullies change."

She saw one of the teachers nod in agreement and felt encouraged. Jamie went on, "Caring for someone and being compassionate for them does not mean you accept their bad choices or their abusive behavior. You don't have to allow them to bully you into joining them or giving in to their demands, as I had once felt. Though it is extremely difficult to stand against someone you are afraid of, turning that fear into confidence allows you to walk away more easily. With the support of others, this group for example, you can reach out to discuss and therefore strengthen your stand. I would like to plan regular meetings and possibly do some stuff together outside of school as well if anyone is interested. Are there any suggestions? Are some days better than others?"

Jamie sat down and joined into a good amount of discussion. Formal meetings were suggested to be held twice a month. It was decided they would take place every other Tuesday at three o'clock. Jamie was hoping this group would become close. After giving out her phone number to all in attendance, Jamie announced that she would like to meet anyone who wanted to attend the Saturday night movie at six fifteen in front of The Rialto Theatre. She then stood to announce the end of the meeting. Her attendees rose and some clapped, expressing their appreciation. As the group filtered out, Jamie was thanked by most, including the teacher that stood over her and Sam that fateful day, the day that had turned her life around.

chapter 29

It was Peter's twelfth birthday. It was a quarter to five, and the table was set for four. Peter was giddy with delight, bouncing off the walls. Judy had a peace about her as she pulled the lasagna out of the oven to cool a few minutes before dinner. She put the rolls in for the short time necessary to bring them to a light golden brown. Salad had been prepared earlier and was already set on the table with an assortment of dressings. Who would have thought a kid would have requested such an elaborate meal? Pizza would certainly have been appropriate for a twelve-year-old's party, but Peter felt the need for a sit-down meal.

Rich arrived a few minutes before five and was met at the door by his son jumping into his arms. Wrapping his arms and legs around Rich, nearly knocking the presents out of his hands, Peter hugged him tightly. Taking the presents from him, Peter ran off to put them with the others in the living room.

Laughing, Judy came to greet him. "Hi, Rich, come on in." She ushered him through the door. "Peter was apparently too excited to have thought of such matters of etiquette."

Rich walked through the door, slowly looking about in curiosity. In her former life, Judy would have been self-conscious, but his concentrated visual perusal had no effect on her now.

He stepped to the painting hung in the entryway. "This is a really nice piece of artwork, Judy."

Judy turned to hide the grin that spread across her face. "Thanks."

Rich looked more intently at the picture before him. "Judy, was this painting done by you?"

She came to stand beside him. "Yes, when I was first dabbling. The meaning is what's significant to me. That's why I hung it there, anyway."

"What is it, the meaning?" Rich asked.

Judy held her hand up to the painting. "I felt like I was representing movement by painting all these intertwined swirls, life's movement or changes. The light and dark represent good and bad times. In some instances, like here,"—Judy pointed to a particular spot on the painting—"this represents the peace God gave me during a difficult time. See, the light is wrapped around a shadow of darkness."

Rich appeared impressed by what he saw.

Jamie leaped down the stairs upon hearing that her father had arrived. "Daddy!" she exclaimed, embracing him tightly.

He kissed her cheek, enjoying the greeting of his once rebellious daughter. "How did your meeting go at school?"

"It was awesome! I hope I can encourage others to be strong and confident too. You know, to not let people get them down. That's my goal, anyway. The people that came listened to my feelings, and they gave some great ideas too."

"That's great, Jamie. It sounds like it went well."

"It did. Sam, the kid I got in trouble over, was there. It was really cool. I feel like I'm doing something important. Oh, and I saw Stephanie. I guess the mean kids are making a 'bully group' just to spite me. Oh well. I'm not worried. I put a face on the enemy." Jamie wandered into the kitchen as Rich looked questioningly at Judy.

"What's that mean, 'a face on the enemy?'" he whispered.

"The enemy is Satan. Just some advice I gave her so she wouldn't get caught up in hating the kids who were bothering her. Hate can be so damaging. That's something God has taught me over time, anyway." Judy also stepped into the kitchen. "Time to eat, everyone!"

They all sat down at the kitchen table together. They enjoyed a wonderful dinner as a family, just as Peter wanted for his birthday.

After dinner the family sat in the living room while Peter opened his presents. He took his time, unlike most kids, savoring the moment. The art set was a hit, as were the books and especially the gift certificate to the museum. Judy looked at Rich when Peter opened it; he smiled back with a wink of thanks for the suggestion.

Rich looked around the living room. It was no longer familiar to him, as it was neat and clutter free. A painting, hung centrally over the couch, completed a well-organized yet cozy atmosphere. He stood to get a closer look at it. The brass plaque tacked to the maple frame read *The Light Within*. He turned to find Judy watching him. As he questioningly gestured to the painting, she came to stand by his side to explain.

"This painting represents the very night God came into my life asking to be first and foremost, at the center of all that I am and all that I do. I don't know if you remember the night, but we had been fighting. Over what I don't even know, but I had left. That picture is a representation of how I felt that night when I was crying in the woods where I had gone to be alone. I felt naked and ashamed. God filled me with his peace deep inside. It was a feeling I can't describe." Rich watched her quietly as Judy continued. "The picture also indicates how he worked on me. He made all the changes in me from the inside. I know it doesn't quite make sense, but I didn't have to try to be something I wasn't anymore."

Rich turned back to the painting and appeared to be deep in thought.

Clearing his throat, he glanced around the room. His response sounded cold. "Hmm, I remember that night. Things were pretty rough between us." Rich awkwardly turned to join their son, who was browsing through his pile of gifts.

Judy watched him, a bit confused by his behavior. It was nice, though, having him there. They did feel so much like family. She took in the sight of Rich, with Jamie and Peter on either side of him, seeming to enjoy the space that used to be home to him. She returned to the kitchen to light the twelve candles on Peter's cake.

chapter 30

It was Saturday night, 6:15 p.m. Judy waved good-bye after dropping Jamie off at The Rialto.

Jamie stood waiting in the cold for others to join her for the movie. She thought about Tracy, a sophomore who had attended the meeting at school. Tracy had called Jamie earlier in the day. She was hoping to come but was unsure if her mother would let her.

Tracy shared quite a bit about the bullying going on in her life, by her mother. Such a call was surprising, but this was what Jamie was hoping to accomplish. If people would reach out for support and healthy encouragement, they just might get through life's ups and downs less scarred and emotionally stronger.

There had been a fight between Tracy and her mother earlier. Jamie helped Tracy step back and work through it.

"What was the fight about?" Jamie asked.

"Nothing really. I guess she thought I had left my dirty dishes on the table. Even though she leaves stuff laying everywhere, she flipped out at me, and it wasn't even me."

Jamie thought of how to respond in a supportive way. She wanted to encourage Tracy to look at this in a new way, a nonjudgmental way. "Hey, let's not get down on your mom. Maybe she's got other things on her mind."

"Yeah, I guess."

"Does she get upset about things like this often?"

"Yup, it just doesn't seem like a big deal to me. So what if it was me? Who really cares?"

"Tracy, do you really want the fighting to stop with your mother?"

"Of course I do."

"Then you have to look at things differently. The only person you can change is you. Try to see the situation from her point of view. Take some time to try that without being mad about it. You might feel differently about her reactions then."

"I guess you're right. I should try something because I'm sick of getting yelled at."

"Talk to her about all this when she's not upset. Ask her what bothers her so much. You might be surprised at her answers."

"Maybe."

"Tracy, are you safe with her?"

"Yeah," Tracy answered quickly, as if she were insulted.

"Sorry, but you know, there's got to be kids who are getting hurt at home. I just had to ask."

"That's okay, I understand. No, I've never felt like she was dangerous, just annoying."

Their discussion had lasted for over an hour. Jamie's spiritual growth had matured her beyond her years and was now reaching past her to touch others.

The cold was nearly unbearable. Jamie was shivering when Sam arrived, joining Jamie on the sidewalk in front of the theater. They were joined shortly by Tracy. Tracy hugged Jamie and thanked her for her encouragement. The talk with her mother had gone well. Five more kids arrived, and the camaraderie was being felt by all as they excitedly waited for the ticket booth to open when a car, careening around the corner, caught their attention.

Stephanie jumped out as the car came to a screeching halt in front of the theater. She grabbed Jamie. "Hurry, get in; get in!"

Jamie was surprised and resisted Stephanie's urgent pull on her arm. "What do you mean? What's going on?"

"Get in; they're coming! Jamie, you have to get out of here. Jim is coming after you!" Stephanie was screaming, and panic was taking control. "We just left the meeting, and he is wicked mad!"

"So what? I'm not afraid of him." Looking at those around her, Jamie felt confident in her stand against evil. Even so, she felt her stomach drop as the sound of a loud exhaust was heard before the truck even came into view. Stephanie, with absolute fear in her eyes, quickly stepped behind Jamie and shoved her into the front seat, slamming the door behind her. She frantically pulled at the back door to get it open and, jumping in, screamed for Taylor, the driver, to "move it."

With tires screeching in protest, Taylor jammed the gas peddle to the floor while Stephanie fumbled to get her door closed.

"What's going on? You can't make me go with you!" Jamie was furious that the choice to stand against her foe was taken out of her hands.

"Believe me, Jamie, you don't want to be there. He's out to get you, and I don't mean that he's gonna pull your little pigtails either." Stephanie turned to look out the back window. "Oh my God, Taylor, get moving! He's coming!"

They raced wildly through the back roads. Jamie and Stephanie buckled up. Taylor sped on, hoping to lose the wickedness that tailed them. Stephanie quickly explained to Jamie what was going on. "We just left the first meeting of The Defects. Jim's mission for the night is revenge on you for ratting us out. He said he is going to make you an example to all who choose to stand up against him."

"I'm sure nothing would have happened. This is crazy. We're going to get hurt. Taylor, slow down," Jamie insisted.

"No, Taylor. Jamie, you don't get it. Since Jim believes your meeting was to target us, his goal is to get you and bring you back to the warehouse. If they get you, the gang is going to strip you naked, beat the crap out of you, and leave you to walk or crawl home if you can."

"Why are you here then and not with them?"

"That was too much. They've gone too far."

"Guys, I'm not sure where to go. I can't shake them." Taylor's voice was shaky. "I'm scared." They had nowhere to hide. Taylor careened around corners and up and over hills. She was searching for a driveway, a house with lights on, anywhere they might be protected. Stephanie kept looking behind. Jim kept his high beams on, bearing down on them when the opportunity arose.

Jamie was watching the truck, baffled by the danger Jim was imposing on them with no sense of conscience evident whatsoever. Could anyone be so hurt and broken, so angry and bitter, that they had no ability to decipher between right and wrong?

The car jerked quickly to the right as Taylor slammed the brakes on. She screamed so loudly it pierced the ears of her companions. Jamie and Stephanie turned to face forward in just enough time to see the legs of a moose in the headlights before them. Within a split second, the large, dark body of a seven hundred-pound bull, legs broken on impact, slammed onto the hood, windshield, and roof of the weaker Toyota Camry. The moose's weight crushed down on the front passengers as the car slid to the side of the road and settled to a stop.

chapter 31

Judy had been getting ready to head into town to wait for the movies to get out when the horrible call came. She dialed Rich immediately. "Rich, meet me at the hospital."

"Are you okay?" Rich's voice was heavy with concern.

"It's Jamie."

"What happened?"

"She's been in a car accident." Judy was chaotically running around the house. She had told Peter to quickly get his clothes back on after he had already gotten ready for bed, and she was now holding his jacket, waiting to leave.

"Where? Who was she with?" Rich's voice sounded cold.

"I don't know." Peter had rushed to his mother's side dressed and ready to go as she helped him get his coat on. "I dropped her off at the movies. I was just getting ready to head back into town to get her when the police called. I'm heading out now. Meet me at the hospital."

"I'm on my way."

Nurses were rushing around the halls of the large hospital, and family members were pacing the waiting room, which was busier than it had been in some time. Though it felt like only minutes had elapsed, time was ticking by quickly.

Judy and Peter were waiting for Rich in the hospital waiting room. Judy was confused. Why a car accident? She had left their little girl at the movie theater entrance. No further information was relayed to her. She had a sick feeling in the pit of her stomach. Peter was silent as he sat beside his mother.

Rich reached the hospital's parking lot in record time and rushed through the doors. Others in the waiting area seemed to be still awaiting information. A nurse had come out and taken a group of people Judy did not recognize with her through a set of swinging doors. As she looked around at the remaining people in the room, she noticed Stephanie's mother. More confusion filled her mind.

Rich had his arm around Judy and held Peter's hand; Judy hadn't noticed that before. Suddenly, an anguished cry was heard from beyond the swinging doors, the sound so pitiful it sent chills down Judy's spine. She looked up into Rich's eyes and saw fear filling them. Shortly, the family that had just been ushered out came back through the waiting room toward the exit. The older woman of the group was sobbing uncontrollably, and a tall, teenage boy was holding her, helping her to the door. A man, unkempt and separate, walked at a distance behind them; a tear escaped his glassy eye.

Judy took a deep breath and looked around for a doctor or nurse to question. There were none present. Something horrible had taken place, and though she did not understand what, why, or how, she sought God's solace. Feeding off the fear in her ex-husband was not going to be helpful to her right now, nor was allowing her own fears free reign. She needed to cling to God, his peace, and a trust in his will.

Stepping out from under the hand of Rich, Judy went forward to face Stephanie's mother. They had never formally met. Judy had waved to her once or twice when dropping Stephanie off, but she had seemed very indifferent and unapproachable then. Judy stood before her now. "Hi, I'm Judy Parker, Jamie's mother. Any idea what's going on?"

"They hit a moose." Her voice was as flat and empty as her eyes. No emotion was evident.

Judy persisted in her search for more information. "I don't understand. I dropped Jamie off at the movies."

Looking Judy in the eyes now, Stephanie's mother slowly responded once again, "They hit a moose."

Judy could smell the booze on her breath and looked around at the others seated nearby. It all felt like a dream, a terrible dream. A nurse entered the room, and Judy rushed to her. "I was called. My daughter, Jamie, has been in an accident."

The nurse brought Judy to the intake desk, where Judy beckoned to Rich and Peter to join her. After clarifying relations, the nurse brought them into a separate meeting room, where a policeman came to join them. Judy's heart was pounding.

"Your daughter is in very bad condition," the nurse began. "They are doing all they can here in emergency to prepare her to go to the trauma ward upstairs. She is being X-rayed as we speak."

"What happened?" Rich asked.

The nurse gestured to the waiting policeman. "Perhaps Officer Rice can explain."

The officer stepped toward them and spoke. "Your daughter was the front passenger in a car that hit a moose. The moose crushed the car, and the young driver died. Your daughter and the backseat passenger were not conscious when we arrived."

Judy shook her head in denial. "Jamie was at the movies." She would never have questioned that. "How did this happen?" She shared her confusion with the officer.

"All I know, ma'am, is that your daughter was not at the movies. She was riding in a car, quite fast, on

REBECCA L. MATTHEWS

Treble Road with two other girls. I am sorry." With that, the officer left the room.

Judy turned her attention to the nurse. "Can we see her?"

"I'll have to check with the doctor. Wait in the waiting room, please, and I'll get back to you." The nurse left the room as well, leaving the family in shock.

Rich's fear began to turn to anger. "It's that Stephanie. Jamie mentioned her again the other day. She's nothing but trouble. I can't believe Jamie would have lied to us like this, but with that girl involved, I see things a bit clearer." Bitterness crept into his voice.

Judy hugged Peter closer as they returned to the waiting room.

Stephanie's family was taken out for an update as well. They returned to the room chatting more than they had been before.

Judy and Rich overheard their discussion. "We'll be able to see her soon, once she is settled into a room." Judy caught the resentful look that Rich was sending their way and prayed for him to have compassion and to let go of the anger that was obviously consuming him.

chapter 32

Many grueling hours later, in the pediatric trauma ward, they were able to see their daughter, one parent at a time. Peter was not allowed in, which was a blessing in disguise. Jamie was not recognizable. Judy stood at her daughter's bedside holding her hand, avoiding all the wires that were snaked around it.

She gazed upon the lifeless body of her child, and a tear slid down her cheek in acknowledgment of the pain that was tearing through her body. "No, no," she whispered, ever so delicately. "No, no." The only thing resembling her daughter, any person for that matter, was the steady beat of her heart, ticking like a metronome, audible via the machinery hooked to her, the machinery supporting her life. Her eyes were swollen shut. Dried blood was caked through the strands of hair that poked out from around the gauze wrapped around her damaged skull. Her cheeks were puffed out, and purple was the most prominent hue visible. Judy could not see the child she, only hours before, had waved good-bye to. She was not here before her. Sadness gripped her, deeply and profoundly. Moving her eyes from her daughter's unrecognizable features, visually flitting past the heart monitor, Judy rested her gaze on the window. Past it in fact, to the heavens dripping with frigid starlight above them. *God, I am so confused. Things were going so well, for all of us. Jamie was finding herself, was becoming such a good example to others. Why did you have to allow this? Why now? Please help us; help me.*

Kissing the hand she had just released, Judy went to the door to allow Rich his time with their child.

"Mom, how is Jamie?" Peter did not clearly understand his sister's condition.

Judy ruffled his head as she looked at him sadly. "Honey, she's not well."

"She'll be better soon, right?"

"No, honey, I'm afraid not." Judy chose not to hide the truth of what she knew, which wasn't much. They had allowed them to see her but had given them very little information—at least, very little that was acceptable.

Two doctors, one of whom had been Jamie's very own pediatrician since she was two, had explained that the trauma to her head was severe. So severe, in fact, that there was no brain activity evident. They stabilized her with equipment but assured them she would never recover or survive on her own. Brain dead, their little girl was gone.

Judy sat in the hall waiting for Rich to face reality as well. She held Peter in her arms, and they cried softly together. She could hear Rich through the door. He sobbed. Low, mournful sounds escaped him, reverberating off the hospital room walls.

When Rich finally appeared at the door, he looked markedly different. Disheveled and forlorn of course, but darker. Judy couldn't quite put her finger on what was so disturbing now about the man standing before her. "Rich, I'm going to take Peter home."

He looked at her but didn't seem to be registering her words.

She and Peter rose. Peter pulled on his mom's sleeve, beckoning her close. "Mom, what's wrong with Dad?"

"He's upset, honey. Let's get home." Turning back to Rich and holding his arm to get his attention, she spoke once more. "Rich, I'm going to take Peter home." Peter needed some rest, and Judy needed to be in a different space, spiritually speaking.

Peter hugged his dad goodnight. Rich wept as he clung to his son. His hold was tight and long. He needed to feel him, to absorb his very life and hold on to it, at least for the moment.

"I'll be back in a few hours, Rich. I need to get someone to stay with Peter at home."

Wiping the tears from his face onto his sleeve, Rich looked up from Peter to his ex-wife. "I'm gonna stay here. There must be something they can do."

"Rich, you heard what the doctors said—"

"No! I can't believe it. There must be something." Rich said adamantly.

Officer Rice rounded the corner and approached them. He had more information about the events of the evening. A nurse was with him; she took Peter for a walk. The adults entered a small room that held a table and chairs. Judy and Rich sat and listened as the pieces of the puzzle fit tighter together.

"Two boys came in to the police department to report that they had witnessed the accident that your daughter was in." Officer Rice hesitated.

Judy and Rich looked at each other. "Okay," Rich said impatiently, wanting to hear what else the officer needed to tell them.

"Apparently the boys were in a vehicle that was chasing the girls before they hit the moose. Do you know the name Jim Davis?"

Judy spoke up. "He is one of the boys that Jamie said bullied a kid named Sam at school."

"He is the leader of a newly formed group he calls The Defects. Did your daughter also form a group at school?"

"Yes, they had just had their first meeting a few days ago, and a group of them were going to the movies tonight together," Judy said.

"Jim's group met yesterday. These boys told me that Jim was very mad your daughter was having these meetings. He felt they were a direct insult to him. He wanted to teach her a lesson and planned to beat her up. Not everyone in his group agreed, however. Taylor and Stephanie went to warn your daughter."

Rich hung his head and covered his face with his hands. "No. No. How could anybody do this to my daughter?"

"Jim has been arrested. The two boys that were with him have agreed to testify against him." Officer Rice stood to leave. "These two boys are really very sorry for having been involved. I am sorry for all of this too." The officer left the room, leaving Rich and Judy to absorb the information alone.

Rich began to cry. Judy walked to the window and gazed out. The oppression was strong, and the horribleness of this moment was nearly unbearable. She remembered a lesson God had taught, and the timing was just right—she needed to fast, not from food, but from fear and worry. She focused on him and talked to him within her heart. His strength was there, and his peace was present for her to cling to.

Rich was becoming more agitated. Judy crossed the room and approached him. She rubbed his arm affectionately, though she was not able to draw his eyes to look into her own. "I'll be back."

Leaving Rich, Judy found Peter at the nurses' station. "Hi, Mom." His words were quiet. He was trying to process everything that was happening around him.

"Hi. Are you ready to go?" Judy held Peter's hand as they walked down the hospital corridors and out the exit to her car. They sat in silence for a few moments, absorbing reality a bit more deeply. They were going home, and Jamie would not be there.

....

Rich wandered the halls, deep in thought and desperately spiteful. In his travels he recognized one of the people he had seen earlier in the emergency room. He was now sitting in the hall, which could only be an indication that Stephanie's room was close at hand. Rich stopped to look through the window nearest the man. He could see Stephanie; she was attached to machines, just as Jamie was. A woman was sitting at her bedside, holding her hand and crying. The scene was quite reminiscent of the one he had just been a part of himself.

Turning to the person sitting beside the door, Rich was still trying to swallow the anger he previously felt toward the teenager behind the glass. "Are you Stephanie's father?" Rich didn't know who Stephanie's parents were. It always bothered him that Stephanie had been dropped off and picked up many times from his apartment but no adult ever came to meet him. *Don't they even care who they are leaving their kid with?*

The man rose. "No, I'm Scott, Regina's boyfriend. Regina is there; she's Stephanie's mother." He pointed through the window.

"Oh. My daughter, Jamie, was in the accident too."

"How is she doing?" Scott inquired softly.

Rich could feel his anger rising. If only he had been a faithful husband, his child would never have rebelled and become friends with Stephanie. They all wouldn't be here today. They would not be dealing with such a horrific tragedy, if only he had kept his vows. Swallowing hard, he answered, "Not well, she's not doing well at all." Shaking his head, he turned, walked away, and returned to the bedside of the child he could no longer hold or comfort.

REBECCA L. MATTHEWS

chapter 33

Judy lay down to rest for a little while after settling Peter into his room. It was nearly three thirty in the morning. She planned to return to the hospital as soon as she could. She and Rich had much to discuss. They needed to talk about taking Jamie off life support, and their pediatrician had brought up the subject of organ donation. Rich had nearly flipped out at the suggestion. He was not able to face the truth of their daughter's condition, not yet anyway. Judy respected that and decided to put such discussions on hold, temporarily.

Lying on her bed and needing to be free of these terrible topics, Judy sought the comfort of her Father. Fasting once more from the all-consuming worry, she focused on God and visualized Jesus there with her, comforting her. Hours later, as the sun was beginning to rise, Judy awoke. Only a few hours of sleep, but the rest her body had needed was met. *Thank you, Father, for holding me through this horrible time. I pray for your strength going forward. I miss my little girl already.* Tears slid down her cheeks. She rose, showered, and dressed.

She made some extremely difficult phone calls to relatives and had Sarah, their old sitter, make plans to come stay with Peter for the day. She couldn't imagine him being alone at a time like this but knew it was best that he not be at the hospital with them.

Once Judy felt comfortable with the things she had accomplished this morning and Sarah had arrived, she went to Peter's bedroom to say good-bye. She was surprised to find him awake and crying. Judy held him. They shared tears, anger, hurt, and even chuckles over good memories. Mostly she just held him; the sensation filled her. She would never take for granted his touch, his words, his smell, or his feelings. She absorbed all that he was. Jamie was a reminder that you may not have tomorrow with the one you love; embrace today.

Once they felt as though they had released all the hurt that was necessary to step forward, at least for this moment, they both climbed out of his bed. Peter got dressed and went to see Sarah, whom he hadn't seen in quite some time. Judy kissed him once again and stepped out the door to return to the hospital. It was nearly ten, and she knew it was time to face her future, painfully different as she knew it would be.

There were two cars parked in front of the house, at the curb. When Judy came down the steps, both cars' doors opened, and passengers tumbled forth in multitude. Six teenagers approached her in the cold morning air, their faces ashen and tear-stained. The gossip had filtered around quickly, giving them bits and pieces of what had happened.

First to speak was a girl Judy did not know. "Hi, I'm Tracy. I spoke with Jamie yesterday on the phone. She was such a help to me and my mom." She gestured to the car as her mother lifted a hand in acknowledgment. "We joined her group at school, and we were with her last night before she left the theater. We are so sorry for what has happened."

"Thank you, Tracy, all of you. I was just going back to the hospital now."

A boy who had stayed at the back of the crowd spoke in a quiet voice. "Is she going to be okay?"

Judy took a shaky breath. "No." Voicing it brought tears to Judy's eyes. She didn't know how much these kids had heard. She wasn't comfortable bearing the bad news but understood how inaccurate rumors could be. Choking back the tears and stopping now and again to regain her composure, Judy gave an account of last night's tragedy as she best knew it.

The boy spoke again. This time he sounded agitated. "It's my fault!"

"That's not true!" Tracy firmly corrected him.

"It all started because of me." He was crying. His face was red from anger, not from the cold.

Judy was filling in the blanks and realized who this must be. "Sam?"

He looked up at her and nodded, tears running down his face.

"Sam, it did not happen because of you. None of this was your fault. In fact, I believe Jamie was trying, by forming this group, to encourage you all to be strong so you don't have to live in fear." The kids nodded in agreement. "She believed that self-confidence gives a strength no bully can bend. She didn't want insecurity, imposed by others, to stop you from living your life." Returning her attention to Sam, Judy continued, "Sam, you didn't do anything wrong; they did. Don't let their actions bully you into feeling responsible. It was right for her to stand up against them. If you have confidence in yourself, you can stand up for what is right too, regardless of the consequences." As Judy was speaking these last words, the clarity of her daughter's message became evident to all. The message was simple; the meaning was profound.

Jamie had accomplished great things. She had accomplished what she had set out to, and God allowed her to be an example to all.

chapter 34

At the hospital, after meeting with Dr. Lang, Judy went directly to Jamie's room. Jamie's room…the words were real, but they were wrong. She wasn't there, Judy was sure of that. Her spirit was with their Father. The vessel was broken and needed to be mourned but also released. It was an odd feeling standing by her body. She supposed it helped that the familiar features were not present. Outside of the chipped fingernail polish she had watched her apply last week, there was nothing here that represented Jamie. The stark white sheet covered the many bruises her lower body had sustained as the weight of the moose had pinned her down. It was the lack of oxygen, ultimately, that had rendered her brain dead.

The doctor reconfirmed to Judy their previous diagnosis. He and another doctor had each run multiple tests at different times; her brain never did respond. He had visited with Rich earlier but could not talk with him about it; Rich was hostile and unable to accept the situation. Suggesting a sedative for Rich, Dr. Lang offered his help if they needed him. He would be at the hospital for the day.

Leaving Jamie's room, Judy found Rich in the cafeteria. He obviously had not rested at all. His eyes were wide and bloodshot. His anger was ever present, as noted by Judy when she sat down beside him.

"I saw Stephanie, you know." His words sounded bitter.

"Any word on how she is?"

"How she is?" Rich raised his eyebrows in question as he glared at Judy.

His irritation confused her. "Rich, you need to rest."

"I need my daughter to get better."

"She's not going to get better. We need to talk, but I think you need to rest first. Come with me." People were staring already. Standing, she pulled at Rich's arm. "Come."

He rose. His eyes empty, he followed her. As they walked together down the corridor, Judy noticed the chapel and, pulling him with her, ducked inside. Instantly the atmosphere was softer as the light filtered through the stained-glass windows, giving the room a gentle glow. The crucifix hanging behind the altar seemed to beckon to them.

Judy went to the altar, turned, and sat down, patting a spot beside her. "Here, sit down, Rich." He sat obediently, and she turned to face him, taking his hands in hers. He began to rub her hands, softly and absentmindedly, up and down. She remembered that he used to do that whenever they held hands long ago. She watched his hands caress hers, and looking up at his face, she saw it was clear he had no idea he was doing it. It was as if he had reverted back in time, years ago, to when the children were very little again.

"Rich." Her voice caused him to turn his attention to her face.

He smiled weakly, looking her face over, and then tears spilled down his cheeks. Judy hugged him. He felt like a child in her arms. "Judy, oh, Judy, what have I done? I am so sorry."

Judy listened in confusion. "Rich, you have not done anything wrong. What do you mean?" Her voice was soft and loving.

"It's my fault." His body lurched with sobs. Only an hour or so earlier, she'd heard another person blame himself for Jamie's death as well.

Putting a finger beneath his chin, Judy delicately raised his face so she could look into it. "Rich, this is not your fault. You can't possibly blame yourself."

"If I hadn't hurt you, if I hadn't strayed from you and my vows to you, this never would have happened. How can you be so calm about me, about Jamie? I hurt you. I had another woman; I left you. You never yelled at me; you never got mad; you never fought. Jamie is gone; our little girl is gone." Rich paused as he shuddered. "If I had never done those terrible things, life would be different now. Jamie would never have had a friend like Stephanie, and we would have her with us right now."

Tears filled Judy's eyes. He said it; he acknowledged that their daughter was gone. That was so important. He needed to acknowledge the present to be able to step forward. She could not, however, believe that he was harboring such pain over his past mistakes. She realized the same rang true for that as well; he needed to acknowledge the past to be able to step forward. "Jamie's accident had nothing to do with anything you did or anything I did. It was her life, and she was God's child, to take when he chose. I am not angry with you. I was dreadfully angry with myself when you left, but God gave me peace."

"Peace. I can't imagine what peace feels like. I have watched you live it for so long now. I struggle every day with what I have done and wish I could feel what I see in you, what I feel when I'm around you. Help me have peace."

"I can't give you peace, Rich. You have to reach out to God and ask for it for yourself, really." He looked at her as if she were crazy. "I told you about the light in me. I painted it, remember? It has to come from within, from God. I do accept Jamie's death. I love her and miss her terribly." Judy stopped for a moment as tears welled up in her eyes. "But I accept that God has called her home to him."

Patting his leg and gaining some composure, she continued, "I accept that you made a mistake. I made many mistakes too. They are forgiven, and we are not paying a price for them. This tragedy of ours is not a punishment. Jamie did wonderful things. It was just her appointed time."

Judy stood up and faced Rich. Closing her eyes and lifting her face to the light from the windows, Judy voiced a prayer softly, "Dear Father, thank you for letting us have Jamie, though that time feels so short. I pray that Rich seeks you because I know that, should he do so, he will find you and experience this peace that passes all understanding. I pray that he understands the depth of the meaning of forgiveness that you gave us through your very own Son's death and resurrection, that he understands that forgiveness is complete. He does not need to stumble over guilt and fear; let him understand that he is free."

Kneeling before Rich, Judy took his hands once more. "Rich, I am going to Stephanie's room. I know you are angry. I pray that you let go of that anger. It is damaging to you. Please, sit here and seek. God is with you, and I trust that he will let you know that." She bent forward and set a gentle kiss on his cheek, and then she turned and left the sanctuary.

Rich crumpled to the floor, completely overwrought with sadness.

chapter 35

Judy had gone to Stephanie's room, but she was not there. The room was vacant, and her mother was not to be found. The nurses' station only informed her that tests were being done. They were not privy to give any more information than that.

She returned to Jamie's room and sat at her side, listening to the methodic pulsing of her heart. She wondered at the deep hurt this accident had caused so many others; she then wondered at the peace only she seemed to feel. Why was she so different? Truly, it didn't seem as though she was suppressing feelings or denying them. She simply had peace with whatever God allowed.

Thank you, Father, for this peace. It's as if I feel nothing really, no highs or lows it seems, which is good. It's like a monotone feeling, very level. It allows me to face our tragedy but not be tormented or blinded by it. It's a blessing. Why me, though?

You have faith like a child.

The statement was made firmly. It was not audible but yet heard very clearly. Judy felt chills crawl up and down her spine, and a small smile tugged at her lips. *Faith like a child.* She had never thought much about it before. Faith, believing completely in something you can't possibly know is real, is that what she was doing? But she knew God was real. He showed himself to her time and time again. He gave her guidance. He changed her. He loved her so much she could do nothing more than bask in it. Of course she would then trust anything he allowed, including taking Jamie home. Who was she to judge his decisions? He knew all—past, present, and future; therefore, his plan could certainly be trusted.

She knew that his strength was hers; she knew that trusting him allowed complete freedom from fear and worry. The results of such a trust were present now as she waited for the father of her children to also make this connection. It was her peace that encouraged freedom for others.

....

It was mid-afternoon when Rich quietly walked in the door to join his ex-wife. She had fallen asleep with her head at Jamie's right hand. Rich stood looking at her in wonder. She was remarkable. During the most tragic events of her life, she encouraged him and loved him. The peace she showed was obviously not an act and therefore could not disappear as events dictated.

The peace she exuded was, as she had explained, God within her.

He knew this now. He had fought with God for hours; he'd argued and thrown his tantrums, and yet God remained, steadfast and loving. As a matter of fact, he had fought with God most of his adult life but hadn't realized it. Judy was right—he couldn't seek her to taste the peace she emitted; he had to plunge into God's waters himself. These living waters soaked into his very pores, and for the first time in his life, Rich felt the peace that could only come from the Holy One.

Rich's eyes wandered to his daughter, and for a moment the unsightly face before him transformed back into the beautiful child she had been only a day earlier. Her features were bright and well defined; he smiled at the vision before it melted away, revealing the lifeless body that needed release. He so much appreciated Judy's patience in letting him reach this point in his own time but knew that was God in her. She followed his perfect direction.

Reaching out, he rubbed Judy's arm. She awoke, a bit dazed, and glanced up at him.

"Hey, how are you doing?" She sounded sleepy and calm. It was a beautiful sound.

With the hint of a pained smile, Rich responded, "I'm much better. Thank you so much, Judy, for being you. You knew what I needed."

"God knew what you needed, not me."

"I am ready to talk about Jamie. It's time for me to let her go."

Judy rose to stand before him. "Are you sure you're ready?"

"I'm sure."

"We have been asked about organ donation. Given the circumstances of her injuries, she is a good candidate. I'm not sure if this is too much for you right now. It just seems the right thing to do."

Rich gazed at the lifeless form of his child. "I know. I remember Dr. Lang asking us to consider it. It just sounds so morbid."

"I'll give you some time to think about it. Sit with her." Judy gestured to the seat at Jamie's side that she had just left. "I'm going to go call Peter, to check on him."

Rich reached out and pulled Judy to himself. He hugged her. Holding her felt good; he needed touch right now. She squeezed tightly, letting him know that he was not alone. They cried briefly. Then, stepping back, she left the room.

Rich came out into the hall half an hour later. Judy was standing by the windows at the end of the long corridor looking out at the cold February day. He approached and stood behind her. "How's Peter doing?"

"He's spending time with Sarah. They hadn't been together for a long time, since I cut back on my hours at work. They were playing Monopoly when I called. I think he's okay."

Rich needed to get to the point, before he was too scared to say it. "I agree it would be the best thing to donate Jamie's organs. She would have wanted it. I know that about her."

Judy turned to face him. Her tears became evident. "Thank you, Rich. I felt so strongly about this but needed you to feel the same." She hugged him once again, and together they sought Dr. Lang to share their decisions as well as ask their many difficult questions.

....

Dr. Lang sat with them and listened intently as the two shared their decision to donate Jamie's organs. They asked many questions, many difficult questions, which he answered with compassion yet with a directness they appreciated. Which organs were expected to be donated? When was she to be considered deceased? When could her body be sent to the funeral home? Would the donee be given their information?

Dr. Lang, after answering all of their questions and preparing them the best that he could, brought a twist into the scenario. He needed to discuss Stephanie with them. In the accident Stephanie had been belted in the backseat. The bulk of her injuries were to her chest. Her ribs had been crushed, and one of her lungs was punctured and torn quite severely. Her heart had also suffered deep bruising. They had stabilized her last night, but over the past twenty hours, she had been deteriorating rapidly. She was not expected, at this point, to survive.

Judy and Rich looked at each other. Rich felt a residual tug of gratification, though in his heart, he knew this reaction was not right.

Dr. Lang continued, "Stephanie has been receiving transfusions due to the internal bleeding. It turns out her blood type and your daughter's are the same."

Rich sat a bit higher and more tensely at these words. He had a sense of where this conversation was going, and he wasn't sure he liked it.

"Given the circumstances, I felt it appropriate to seek your permission. With further testing, Jamie's heart and lungs may be a perfect match for Stephanie. Would you agree to donate them to her? We may have a chance at saving Stephanie's life—Jamie may have a chance at saving Stephanie's life."

Rich stood up quickly. His internal reaction was strong.

Judy reached out to touch Rich's arm and quickly spoke up. "Doctor, let us talk alone about this for a minute."

Dr. Lang left the two alone.

Rich was pacing, and Judy sat still, letting him roll with his emotions.

Judy's silence filled the air. Rich's mind was racing. He scanned each reaction, each thought, each emotion as they presented themselves fleetingly through his mind.

He mumbled as he paced. Judy did not judge, nor did she guide. She had confidence in whatever the outcome would be. She would accept any result here because she knew who really was in control.

After some time, Rich returned to the table to face Judy. "What do you think?" He had run his vindictive train to the ground and was open to hear opposing views, which he was sure he would hear from her.

"You said it yourself. This is what Jamie would have wanted," Judy kindly stated. "Do you know how she felt about the group she was forming? She was hoping to reach the very bullies themselves. She was sure that if they could believe they were worth something, they would find strength within that could set them free. Free from the abuse that defined them. Free to be wonderful members of society. What better way to offer that hope than to give life."

Rich sat absorbing his daughter's words, spoken through her mother. The strength they both had shared was infectious. He prodded God in his mind. *Help me to understand. Help me to give as selflessly as these women in my life have given.*

With only a moment's hesitation, Rich agreed. They found Dr. Lang again. He had been preparing the organ donor paperwork for them to sign. With their decision to help Stephanie declared, the doctor began the process of testing for further compatibility. The pair returned to spend their last hour with their daughter.

Family members Judy had called that morning, from both sides of the family, had arrived and were milling around the hallway. Judy and Rich, united, had gone out to share Jamie's condition and their decision, thanking them all for being there for them. They called Peter and shared their decision with him but felt strongly he should not see her in the condition she was in. Judy explained to him she would be home late and assured him she would be there to see him in the morning.

Dr. Lang gave them the news. "They are a near perfect match. We can prepare her for surgery when you are ready."

"The chaplain is coming. We are going to have a brief ceremony. Then we will be ready," Judy explained, squeezing Rich's hand tighter.

Dr. Lang left to prepare Stephanie and her family.

When the chaplain arrived, all of Jamie's family members filed into her small hospital room. There was sobbing heard throughout the crowd. Judy and Rich remained close. Rich caressed her hand again. They were united and both at peace.

chapter 36

Judy and Rich worked to gather items for Jamie's funeral. They sat in Judy's living room together over the next couple of nights, browsing any and all information they had saved since her birth. Peter, obviously missing his sister, spent a lot of time looking at all the memorabilia spread out around him.

After such a night as this, Judy retreated to her sanctuary alone. She hadn't visited this space, really visited it, since before Jamie's accident. Having gone through Jamie's room in the process of pulling together an accurate display of who she was, Judy had found a journal. She took this moment to snuggle onto the loveseat in her room and read her daughter's words.

Just seeing her handwriting and reading through the hurt she had felt while being bullied broke Judy's heart. She cried and continued her reading through the tears. She smiled at the turnaround in her daughter's heart as she accepted God's will in her life. She could sense the great transition in the excitement of her next passages. Judy chuckled at the dream Jamie recounted, of her standing before a packed auditorium announcing the first meeting of The Steadfast United.

The journal ended in mid-thought, so it seemed. Life had turned around, fear had abated, but then the pages that continued were empty. The message did not end, however; it would be carried forward. God had a plan.

Judy put the journal down; she rose and wandered about her room, looking at the snapshots on the wall. Jamie had been so beautiful. Something caught her eye as she turned to get ready for bed—her easel. Stepping around to face the painting last propped upon it, Judy burst into tears. It was the painting of Peter and Jamie. The light shone from them; the likeness was so realistic but deeper—it was spiritual.

....

"Thank you so much for coming." Judy shook hands with many, many people.

"I'm sorry for your loss." These words meant to comfort them were repeated time and time again.

The embraces were tight, and the tears were free-flowing. The funeral of a teenager was difficult to attend.

Jamie's urn was placed on a pedestal near the altar. It was flanked on one side by her school picture, blown up in size, and on the other side by the portrait painted by Judy. Peter sat in front of them and remained there staring at her even after the service was over.

The ceremony at the church was very nicely done. Judy liked Pastor Ryans. She had attended his church on Sunday morning to hear him speak, and she and Rich had met with him a few times to work on funeral arrangements. Their talks always turned to God's love and peace, and they were so uplifting. He was a blessing at such a time as this.

Now, as the people were leaving the church, Judy went to kneel at Peter's side. "Honey, it's almost time to go. Are you okay?"

Peter looked at her. His eyes were swollen and red from crying, and his sleeves were wet from wiping away the tears. "I miss her, Mom."

"I know, honey, I do too." Judy turned and embraced him. They cried together.

Rich joined the pair. He knelt down and wrapped his arms around the two of them together and let his tears fall on his son's head. Judy could feel the family connection. The love here was strong. God was with them.

"Mom…" Peter's soft voice broke through. "Dad, I was listening to the pastor talk about God and Jesus and all." Peter turned his tear-streamed face toward his mother. "I hear you talk about them a lot too, Mom, I've been sitting here talking to him for a while myself."

"That's a good idea, honey. He is there for you whenever you need him."

"Yes, he is. I just learned that myself," Rich added.

"I asked him why he took Jamie away 'cause I miss her a lot, you know." Peter sniffled back a tear. "I think he took her because he loves her and wants to be with her now. I understand. She is a lot of fun to be with." Judy reached for Rich's hand as they listened to Peter finish. "I told him that it is okay and to please make sure she is happy."

The couple once again embraced their son and let the tears flow. This time the tears were in thanks to God. Peter was going to be fine.

chapter 37

The funeral had only been two days earlier. The frantic chaos had suddenly come to a stop, and in that quietness Rich and Judy were sitting having a cup of coffee when there was a knock at Judy's door.

She answered it and found Sam and Tracy standing on the porch. "Come in. How are you both?"

Tracy answered first. "Fine, thank you."

"I'm good," Sam followed up shyly.

Rich stepped into the entryway from the kitchen after hearing the kids' voices. "Hi, guys."

"Hi," they said in unison.

Judy smiled at them. "What brings you around?"

"We want to talk to you about holding another meeting. We have been talking and think that Jamie's group should keep going."

"Wow. I have been so busy." Judy looked at Rich. "Between the accident and the funeral, I hadn't even thought about the group." Returning her attention to the pair, she continued, "Of course, I think that's a great idea."

"If you don't mind, we would like to have it on Tuesday after school. Can you come? We really want you both there."

They all followed Judy as she stepped into the kitchen to check her wall calendar. "Yes, I can make it. Rich, do you want to go too? Does that day work for you?"

"Yes, I'll take the time off. I think continuing it is important," Rich said.

"Okay. We have something else to ask you then." Tracy appeared a bit nervous now.

Sensing the importance of the discussion, Judy pulled out a couple of chairs. "Have a seat, kids." Both Rich and Judy joined them at the table.

Tracy took a deep breath after looking at Sam, who was nodding to her in encouragement. "Tim and Derek, the kids who were in the truck with Jim, are asking to speak at the meeting."

Judy and Rich looked at each other in shock. "You've got to be kidding," Rich said.

"Well, that's what I thought until they talked about it more. Think about it. Jamie's message was to help people make good choices, not let people bully them into bad situations. These two are the perfect example of the bad that can happen when you don't do that."

Judy thought about that for a minute then nodded in halfhearted agreement. "I guess I see that point."

"Here's another point. They want to talk about how they were treated when they were little. Apparently they agree with Jamie's philosophy that bullies were probably bullied themselves. They want to shed light on that perspective from their own experiences."

Rich was quiet as he listened. Judy looked to him, wondering what he thought. *Would this be too much?* she wondered. "They have been suspended from school because of their involvement in the accident, right?"

"Yes, we'd have to talk to the principal first, of course," Sam answered.

Judy looked at Rich again. "Let us think about it." She rose from her seat and got a piece of paper. "I'll call you tonight, Tracy. Give me your number."

....

The meeting was scheduled to be held in the library, but the number of students showing up to attend filled the room, spilled out the door, and clogged the hallways. Judy was amazed and excited. Mr. Plante, the principal, had no other choice but to move the meeting to the auditorium. The students waited patiently while the stage was set up to be used as the platform for the speakers.

While the principal connected a microphone and brought out the podium, Judy set up her easel to display the painting of her children. She wanted Jamie's image to be present for all her members to see. She was, after all, the founder of this newly formed organization. Judy looked at the crowd as they waited in quiet anticipation of the message about to be given. She recognized many faces from the funeral and felt a pride well up within for what her daughter had begun.

Tracy stood at the podium first. "I would like to welcome you to the second meeting of The Steadfast United. We are committed here to supporting one another without judgment. As Jamie had suggested, we believe that unconditional support can only encourage an inner strength. Therefore, no bully, no abuser, nobody can make you feel worthless. Openly sharing your concerns and fears, your difficult situations, your intimidations, in Jamie's opinion, would allow you to be free from them. We want to continue her legacy and continue to offer that same support. Sam wanted to say a few words as well. Thank you." As Tracy stepped aside, the people in the auditorium applauded.

Sam stepped to the microphone next. "As you may know, I am very shy. That's probably why I am picked on so much. It was Jamie who stood up to the people who have picked on me the most, even though it meant that she got in trouble. It also led to why she is not here today." Sam choked on tears that suddenly welled up; audience members began wiping their own faces. "Jamie made me realize that nobody has the right to make me feel bad about myself. She helped me to understand that I am fine just the way I am. I am proud to be a part of her organization. Thank you."

From backstage Judy brought the next speakers into view. Tim and Derek approached the microphone. The audience, as a whole, gasped. Shouts of anger were heard; threats were tossed about.

Judy quickly went to the microphone to hush the crowd. "What are we offering here in this group? Judgment? To stay true to Jamie's memory, we must be open to hear what these two have to say. You may accept them or not, but tolerance is expected." The crowd hushed once more as Judy stepped aside. "Go ahead, boys."

"Hi, my name is Tim, and this is Derek, in case some of you don't know us. We were in a truck chasing Taylor, Stephanie, and Jamie when they had their accident."

Chatter arose from the crowd. Tim waited for the murmurs to subside. Soon the crowd hushed once more.

"'Bullies.' That is what most of you think of us, and that is what we have spent our lives being. The accident made us see that about ourselves too. We want to share with you who we really are. Both Derek and I have families that aren't very nice to us; we're hated, screamed at, and smacked around a lot. Always have been. This is not our excuse; this is a lesson, for all of you. Jamie was right in what she believed, and what she has offered is good. Like her posters said, support and acceptance of each other can help you be strong. It can help you to stand up for good, even when bad may be happening to you. We took our anger and hatred out on many of you guys; it didn't make us feel any better. It wasn't until we talked about it, with each other, with someone who didn't judge, that we both realized we wanted to be free of the hurt and anger we were holding on to. Standing here in front of you is our attempt to help others make better choices, and by supporting Jamie's message, we think we can do that."

Tim turned to Derek to offer him time to speak. "There are many of you here that are hurting inside too, many whose parents fight or whose parents are drunk or drugged and don't care. Some of you are even being abused and are hiding it. You may not act out like we did, but keeping your hurt inside keeps you as insecure as we were. We followed a bully. We gave in to him because we were scared, and look at what happened. Don't give in to your bullies. You are worth more than that. Talk to someone. Don't let your insecurities make your decisions for you. I'm very sorry for much of what I have done." Derek looked down at his hands. Then he raised his eyes once more. "Thank you for listening."

The applause was thunderous. Tim and Derek went to Rich, Judy, and Peter and, though their words were nearly drowned out by the crowd behind them, humbly apologized. Judy hugged them and through tears thanked them for their words of wisdom. Rich shook their hands, though he had to admit he was terribly torn inside on how to feel about these two boys.

Judy held hands with Rich and Peter. Together they walked to the podium, and she spoke. "I want to thank all of you for being here. I want to thank each of these speakers today as well. I feel it is very important to make the point that Jamie's goal has been achieved. She had walked these halls in fear after making a wise choice to stand up for what was right. Realizing that fear was being used to manipulate her, she decided to look at the situation differently. She chose to have compassion on her enemies, and realizing the freedom that brought, she wanted others to experience the same. She also wanted to encourage people to set boundaries. It is okay to care for someone, even if they have mistreated you, but you should never allow their mistreatment of you to continue or to let them compromise your belief in yourself. Jamie's goal was to bring confidence to each and every one of you so that you can stand up for what is right, but her goal became much more far-reaching than that. She wanted the very bullies that harassed her to gain this same confidence too so they could also be free from the harm that had been brought to them. Her death was not in vain. By the very speeches these two young men just made, we are all a witness that the bullies within the halls of this school have been effectively disarmed. Freedom not only will reign here, but, because of her, it will reign in them as well."

Judy, Rich, and Peter went backstage and hugged tightly. From their positions they could hear Tracy discuss future plans, request suggestions and ideas, and then bring the meeting to a close. Cheers were heard throughout the halls of the school—cheers from the new members of The Steadfast United.

The three bowed their heads in prayer as the meeting adjourned. "Thank you, Lord, for what you have done here."

Rich took Peter back to his place for the night since Judy wanted to remain behind at school with Sam and Tracy. They had a lot to go over.

A gentle tug on her sleeve beckoned Judy to turn around.

"Hi, I'm Regina, Stephanie's mother. I came here to thank you." Regina's eyes were swollen from crying. "You saved my daughter's life."

Sam and Tracy ducked away, leaving the two women to talk in private.

Judy was happy to see Regina. "How is Stephanie doing?"

"She is still in critical condition, of course, but she seems to be doing much better, thanks to you and your family."

"It's what Jamie would have wanted. How are you doing?" Judy remembered their meeting in the emergency waiting room. Regina had seemed intoxicated and incoherent, though it could have been the shock of the news they had all received that had her so disengaged.

"I'm struggling, I guess. I listened to what you all were talking about in the auditorium. I'm afraid I have not been a good mother myself."

Judy reached out and held her arm. "We all make mistakes as parents, but the important thing is to acknowledge them. Something I've learned is that exposing the bad somehow seems to help change it."

"I got that from what you all were talking about. You must have been an awesome mother to Jamie. Your son is so lucky."

Judy chuckled. "Actually, I was mean and disrespectful to my kids for many years—to my husband too. It was only a couple of years ago that God touched my life and changed my heart. The kids responded wonderfully to that, but I am far from perfect still."

"God, hmm…He wouldn't care to touch my life. I've screwed up so much. I wouldn't even dare step foot in a church; I'm sure I'd be struck by lightening."

"Regina, God loves us no matter what. Often we struggle with consequences of our own actions, not his punishment. And you don't need to go to any church to meet up with him; he's here where you are, anywhere you are, waiting for you to just ask him to help you and guide you." Not expecting to get so preachy, Judy changed the subject back to Stephanie. "You may be getting a second chance with Stephanie, you know. If you say you've been a bad mother, maybe this is your chance at something better, for both of you. I dare say, though, that you can't do it alone." Judy felt herself returning to the preaching and hesitated.

Regina looked defeated. "I do need help, don't I?"

"I can only offer advice from my own experiences. Understand I am no better than you; I'm just a person trudging through this world as well. I don't believe you can change yourself, I mean *really* change. That is too great a job for any of us. When I asked God in, I had to step back to let him make the changes in me. At times I was frustrated, at times I was impatient, but it was really amazing to see what he could do in me." Judy felt excited, and the twinkle in her eye seemed to catch Regina's attention. She really believed in what she was saying, and it showed. "Regina, I believe God is big enough to help you. If you want him to, all you have to do is ask. You are welcome to call me anytime, though, you know. After all, supporting one another is what we are encouraging here."

When Regina left, Judy went to the library, where she found Sam and Tracy talking. She joined them, and they continued their discussions about the organization.

They spent hours outlining their philosophy, creating ideas for upcoming meetings, and hashing out thoughts on social gatherings for their members. Judy had obtained paperwork from the state they had to complete to make it an official nonprofit organization. Unexpectedly, many donations had flooded in on behalf of both Taylor and Jamie, all for the group that Jamie had been forming.

The tasks before them were great but so worth any amount of time and energy they were to spend on them. Jamie had no idea what she had begun; God's power and wisdom had worked through her, and her death had compelled the importance of her message into extremely grand proportions.

chapter 38

Over the months following the death of Jamie, Judy and Rich spent a lot of time together. In a concerted effort to help Peter cope with the severe changes the loss of his sister represented, they did many things together as a family. The boundaries previously made by weak, earthly thinking that had kept Judy and Rich at a decided distance were no longer present.

The Steadfast United meetings and social events, as well as dinners, movies, and family game nights with Peter, kept Judy and Rich in close physical proximity. Spending much of their free time together, they were quickly becoming the very best of friends.

Inevitably, God and his intimate and personal connections, though experienced differently by both, became exciting topics of conversation for Rich and Judy. They loved to share what he was doing in their lives and the guidance they often would feel from him. They had not met many others who had chosen to follow such a personal relationship with God, and the awe of it made for wonderful discussions.

Idle gossip, fights, and complaints of an earlier life were long forgotten, replaced by laughter, unconditional support, and uplifting visits that lasted sometimes into the wee hours of the morning. Respect replaced judgment and condemnation in the hearts of the pair.

Summer had passed, a new school year was well underway, and the holidays were now nearing a close. It was Christmas Eve, the most precious time of the year for this threesome. Rich was preparing to return home, having helped wrap Peter's gifts and settle him in to bed for the night.

"I can't believe so much time has passed since Jamie left us. Tomorrow is Christmas morning. I miss her. It will feel strange without her sitting around the tree with us." Judy, from her position on the floor, looked up at Rich. "Can you get here early, maybe around six?"

As the Christmas tree lights danced on her beautiful features, Rich smiled. "Judy, I'd be happy to be here even earlier if you need me to." Rich, understanding Judy's feelings, wanted so much for her to feel comforted.

"I don't know. I have a peace about Jamie; I really do. I trust everything God has done and will do. It's just that I can't imagine Christmas morning without her. I'll be okay, I know."

They walked together to the door, and Rich gave Judy a hug. He held her tight, and she cried lightly on his shoulder.

"Judy, I'll see you in the morning. Merry Christmas." Kissing her on one cheek and wiping a tear from the other, Rich stepped out the door.

He drove home deep in thought and prayer. Wiping the tear from her cheek had reminded him of the day in his office when he felt he couldn't due to his own failures. He had grown so much since then. His failures were forgiven. God had brought him freedom. With such a great gift as this, he had to seek God's wisdom now. He felt led in a new direction but wanted to be sure it was God's will and not his own desires. He went to bed knowing God would make clear his uncertainty.

At two in the morning Rich awoke. Something powerful had awakened him, yet nothing was evident. Was it a noise or a dream? He sat and pondered briefly but knew what to do. He rose and dressed and gathered the presents he had purchased and wrapped for Judy.

Arriving at Judy's house at three in the morning, he knocked lightly. Nobody answered, of course. He quietly let himself in with the key he still had, having used it many times before while watching Peter. He turned on the Christmas tree lights, placed Judy's presents under the tree, set a pot of coffee brewing, and went up the stairs to her room. The door was slightly open, and he could hear her softly crying into her pillow. He crossed the room and sat on the edge of her bed, reaching a hand over to caress her back. "Judy, it's gonna be okay."

Surprised, Judy sat abruptly. She turned and buried her head in his neck; Rich's arms engulfed her with his strong embrace. She continued to cry, now uninhibited. They stayed for a long time in this manner until Judy was done. "Thanks, Rich. You couldn't have had better timing."

"The timing wasn't mine; it was God's. He woke me up and led me here."

Judy chuckled as she wiped her cheeks. With bloodshot eyes, she looked at him as a stray tear slipped free.

Rich reached up, wiped it away, and, feeling compelled, kissed where it had been. "Judy, we need to talk."

A hint of alarm flickered on Judy's face. "Okay, what's up?"

"God has put this on my heart for a time now, and I think it is the right time to discuss it with you. I'm so happy to have you as my best friend. I couldn't imagine this walk with Christ without you. I know it might sound strange to you, but…" Rich pulled a small present out of his coat pocket. "Here, open this."

Judy took the present from his hands and slowly unwrapped the colored Christmas paper from around it. Opening the tiny box now free of its wrapping, she saw the engagement ring she had returned to him when they divorced. Judy's heart began to race wildly.

"I believe, with Christ at the center of us, we would make a great couple, a great family. Will you marry me?"

Judy threw her arms around him and held tight, tears flowing once again. "Yes, yes, yes. Of course, I would love to marry you." Throwing her head back to look to the heavens, Judy rejoiced, "Thank you so much, God!"

The smile could not be taken from Judy's face, and their family Christmas was one of the most blessed days they had ever experienced.

epilogue

By the one-year anniversary of the accident that took the lives of Jamie and Taylor and forever altered the life of Stephanie and many others, a lot of changes had taken place.

Teenagers from the school were changing their relationships with their parents, changing their relationships with each other, bonding, growing, and enjoying healthier, happier lives. Parents were enjoying the kids they had been so frustrated raising, learning from their own children how to be respectful and tolerant. Though the school's atmosphere benefitted from Jamie's efforts, it did not stop there. The home lives of many were positively affected as well.

Stephanie's body accepted the gift her friend had given her. Though she would be medicated the rest of her life, her prognosis was great. She felt very bad about the events that had taken her friends from her, but the effects on her family and home life were profound. With Judy's unending support, Regina handed her life to God and chose to trust in his guidance. This guidance led her in directions she had never been strong enough to take in the past. With boundaries set and a love for herself she had never felt before, Regina kicked her boyfriend out. She and her daughter were worth far more than the abusive treatment they had received for years at his hands. Though she loved him, he had no respect for them or their safety.

The Steadfast United, with Tracy as president, Sam as vice president, and Judy and Rich as advisors, spread like wildfire. Thirty other schools adopted their philosophy and had The Steadfast United come to many speaking engagements. Reaching even deeper, in an effort to help the children most likely to become trouble, the teachers in the grade schools of these districts incorporated what they were learning from Tim and Derek into their plans. They accepted that they should see these children differently, understanding that what happened at home couldn't possibly stay at home. The abusive and demeaning behavior experienced by some needed to be acknowledged so these children could be free to feel and express love themselves. The school districts also chose to reach out to the families of these at-risk students in unique ways, offering them compassion and support, encouraging them in the difficult roles they were having trouble playing.

Tim and Derek testified at Jim's trial, and having been eighteen at the time of the accident, Jim was sentenced to prison. There he joined his father, who had been sentenced three years earlier for aggravated assault. He had thrown acid on the face of his ex-girlfriend, causing her to be permanently maimed. Jim, much like his father, never showed any remorse for the crime he had committed.

Finally, Judy, Rich, and Peter chose the one-year anniversary of Jamie's death to become reunited as a family. The death of their daughter was tragic, but it also brought many positive changes to so many lives. They wanted this day to be memorialized in a special and loving way and believed their wedding was the ultimate way to do so. They had spent the year since her death falling deeply in love. It was a love that was pure, respectful, and unconditional, a love they had never shared before and could not have until Christ was first and foremost at the center of them both.